last night in
Laguna

USA TODAY BESTSELLING AUTHOR
C.M. ALBERT

The unauthorized reproduction or distribution of this copyrighted work is illegal. Criminal copyright infringement (including infringement without monetary gain) is investigated by the FBI and is punishable by up to five years in federal prison and a fine of $250,000. Please purchase only authorized electronic editions and do not participate in, or encourage, the electronic piracy of copyrighted materials. Your support of the author's rights is appreciated. This book is a work of fiction. Names, characters, places, and incidents are the products of the author's imagination or used fictitiously. Any resemblance to actual events, locales, or persons—living or dead—is entirely coincidental.

LAST NIGHT IN LAGUNA

Genre: Contemporary Romance

Copyright © 2016 by C.M. Albert | Flower Work Press

Original cover by Zoe York for the Laguna Kindle World

Updated cover by Marisa Rose Wesley of Cover Me Darling LLC

Book design by Inkstain Design Studio

Editing by Erin Servais of Dot and Dash LLC

All rights reserved. Except for use in any review, the reproduction or utilization of this work, in whole or in part, in any form by any electronic, mechanical, or other means now known or hereafter invented, is forbidden without the written permission of the author.

Last Night in Laguna is dedicated to my father, George F. McCarey, who passed away on July 4, 2000, after a too-short battle with ALS. He was my inspiration for this story and is the reason it's set on the Fourth of July. It is also dedicated to my cousin, Joe McCarey, who is heroically fighting brain cancer. I love you. Please never lose hope.

acknowledgements

This book would not have been possible without a team of amazing people. Behind every great author is a team, and I'm blessed to be working with one of the best groups of people in the self-publishing industry.

My biggest appreciation goes to author Kaira Rouda for continuing to let me use elements of her Laguna Beach series in this book, even after our fun together in her Amazon Kindle World was over. Thank you for letting me borrow Josh, Madison, Annie, and Hank for a spell.

I'd also like to thank author and designer Zoe York for creating the original beautiful, swoon-worthy cover, and Marisa Rose Wesley of Cover Me Darling LLC for helping update it after it came out of the Kindle World program. Thanks for bringing it to life so I could hold my baby in my hands finally! And huge heaping of thanks go to Nadège Richards for making the inside look just as pretty as the outside. She is simply a genius and one of the coolest ladies I know.

Mad love and appreciation goes to my amazing editor, Erin

Servais of Dot & Dash, LLC. Where would I be without you? (Please don't answer that!) Thanks for keeping me honest with my commas. I adore you. (And any remaining errors are my own.)

Many thanks to my dear friend Kenya Moore, owner of The Book Nymph PR. She is always there for me in a pinch when I need a cover reveal, blog tour, or any other PR/Marketing help with my books. I couldn't do this without all of your advice, knowledge, tips, and smiles. You keep me sane!

Big warm hugs sent out to my amazing Colleen's Angels Street Team and Beta Reading Squad for your wonderful feedback as I was originally developing this story. Special thanks this go-around to Alicia, Beth, Cody, Erin, Gwen, Jen, Kate, Kim, Phylis, and Rorie. I adore you ladies and appreciate your time and energy to help make my stories be the best they can possibly be.

And finally, the other pieces of my heart: Derek, Evan, and Gillian. Your love, support, enthusiasm, and belief in me are more than I could ever dare hope for in this lifetime. You are my everything, and I hope you are proud of me for chasing my second dream. You, my loves, are always my first.

"I am homesick for a place I am not sure even exists.
One where my heart is full. My body loved.
And my soul understood."

—MELISSA COX

last night in
Laguna

chapter One

"You guys are the best friends a girl could ever ask for," Bexley yelled over the steel drum band playing on the loosely roped-off porch right outside the restaurant's front door. LagunaMatata was Bex's favorite local bar, so off the beaten path as it was. She waved her hands over her head, her fingers finding a seductive rhythm to match the slow reggae version of a Janoskians song.

She pulled Madison by the hand into the small circle of warm bodies pressed together on the beach. Annie followed her friends, nursing the one piña colada she'd allow herself to indulge in at Bex's goodbye get together.

"Whoa . . . real girls eat cake!" Bex sang in unison with the other partygoers as she jumped up and down without a care in the world. She spun around and inhaled the balmy ocean air. This she would miss. Being around her closest friends. Living in walking distance to the beach. Fresh fish tacos. The bluffs.

It was early yet, the sun still descending; she was putting on a show for Bex's last night in Laguna, firing off her most vibrant oranges and pinks like a belly dancer calling for attention with one last gyration of her hips. "Come on, you two," Bex said, parting her way through the shorts-clad beach bodies so they could make their way to the shoreline. "I don't want to miss my last sunset in Laguna."

Annie handed Bex the bottle of Una Mas she'd carried for her from the bar. "Thanks, doll," Bex said as she dropped onto her butt in the warm sand. The sound of sea gulls and the crashing waves against the huge bluffs down the shore calmed and connected Bex in a way that few sounds did. But as much as this beach grounded her, she was a gypsy at heart and New York was calling.

"What am I going to do without you girls?" Bex asked, watching as Annie sat down to the left of her on the sand, careful to slide her long maxi dress under her bottom. Her friend lifted her coconut to her lips and sipped slowly from the festive red, white, and blue straw.

"Let's not worry about that tonight," Madison said. "Let's enjoy your last Fourth of July in Laguna. If I think too much about you not being in walking distance from me anymore, I will seriously lose it."

Bexley leaned in and placed her head on her friend's shoulder. Their friendship had been quick to develop, but it was a lasting one. Sometimes soul mates came in the form of friends, and Madison Alcott was Bex's long-lost sister at heart. She was what Bexley would miss the most about Laguna Beach.

"Let's not talk about it then. Let's have the funnest night of our lives and send me off with a bang! Speaking of a bang . . ."

Madison arched an eyebrow in Bex's direction as if afraid of what was to follow. Bex heard Annie snicker from her other side.

"I was just going to ask if Josh and his friends would get here by the time the fireworks started. Sheesh! Get your minds out of the gutter, ladies."

"Yeah, he said they would. The nanny already has Francie tucked in for the night, but Josh had to sign off on some big investment deal, so he said he was running a little late. But he wouldn't miss tonight for the world."

"Ew. He has to work on the Fourth of July?" Bex screwed up her face, her normally vivid green eyes shadowed by her furrowed brows. "I hope that's not my future after the move," she said and sighed as she leaned forward to place her chin in her hands, her elbows propped up on her knees.

"So, have you secured a flat in New York, yet?" Annie asked.

Madison gave her a pointed look, peering over Bex in the

process. "Didn't we just say we wouldn't talk about this tonight?"

Bexley laughed. "I guess that's a little impractical, huh?" She sunk her toes deeper into the sand, covering them with the pale beige granules. It was still toasty from the afternoon heat and comforted Bex, reminding her of all the times she'd spent lying on this very beach under the warm rays of the California sun. She noticed the tan line from her sandals and realized that would be a thing of the past in New York. "Actually, the place I was considering fell through, so I'll be crashing with my sister until I can find a new apartment—which, trust me, won't be soon enough."

"I thought you and your sister got along well? Isn't that why you're moving all the way across the country to help her?"

"We do, don't get me wrong," Bexley said, her gaze wandering to the ocean's surface as the last fire-orange hue slipped behind the eternal horizon. *Nothing gold can stay.*

Bexley stood, while offering her hand to Annie. "She's just painfully OCD with her things. You should see her apartment. Not so much as a piece of paper out of place. Can you just see *me* in there? Hurricane Bex, living with someone who folds the end of her toilet paper rolls in a point so they look pretty for guests." She snorted as Annie stood up beside her, Madison pushing up from her seated position too.

"Hey, let's walk down to the cove one last time," Bex pleaded. "We'll get back in time for fireworks, and before Josh gets here."

Madison looked at her watch, uncertainty clouding her eyes. "How about halfway down and back? I don't want to miss them in this crowd."

"Madison, the beach is completely flat. Even if we aren't back yet, we won't miss the fireworks."

"I meant the guys; but thanks for the vote of no confidence," Madison said, laughing.

"So, who is Josh dragging along this time? Another ego monster wannabe actor?" Bexley asked.

"Hey, that's not nice. He has really changed, you know."

Bexley leaned in and hugged her friend. "Oh, sweetie, I know. I didn't mean to imply Josh was! I know he's so over that now." She spun around Madison in the sand, holding one of her friend's hands over her head as she twirled playfully. Bexley's little floral skirt flared out around her, bringing a smile to her lightly tanned cheeks. "I just know that some of the crowd Josh has kept in the past can be a little . . . high maintenance."

"This guy's not like that," Madison insisted. "He's a middle school music teacher. As a matter of fact, it's Josh's cousin, Kai."

Annie batted her eyelashes at Bexley. "Oh, girl. You're gonna have a hard time ignoring Kai; trust me on this one." She flicked her fingers out in front of her as if to say, *too hot to handle*.

"Good thing I'm not in the market and am leaving tomorrow," Bexley pointed out as they made their way down the beach. The crowd thinned as they rounded the corner and the gentle sand gave way to small pebbles. They slipped their sandals off and held them in their hands as they walked lazily through the shallow surf heading toward the bluffs and their hidden cove.

"Oh, and they're picking up Hank along the way. You did get a babysitter, right, Annie?" Madison asked.

"I left it in Hank's court. I told him if he wanted to get laid, he'd better find a sitter and get his cute butt out for the night."

Bex high-fived Annie and then took a slow sip of her beer as she gazed off into the distance where the cove was tucked into the towering bluffs.

"Hey, Bex, you okay in there?" Bex nodded, so Madison pressed on. "So, when do you start work? It's going to be a huge adjustment," she acknowledged gently.

Bexley let out a heavy sigh. It would be. Though she had a communications degree from Sacramento State, she'd been a certified massage therapist for almost the entire six years after college. In fact, it's how she'd met Madison.

"I'm going to miss seeing you every day at work, Mads," she said affectionately. She'd loved working for Madison at the Mondrian resort's spa. Going on nearly a year, it was the longest she'd held a job in any one place. It just wasn't in her nature to let things get too settled. She was made for change and movement—a gypsy heart is what her parents had told her when she was young and they were still alive. Hell, they'd instilled it in her from the very beginning, shuffling the family around from town to town up and down the West Coast while she and her sister Vaughn were growing up. Bexley inherited her wanderlust from their dad.

"You have the heart of a gypsy, the soul of a poet, and the attention of a gnat, my little Bexie Bean," her father would say. She choked back her tears. She refused to cry tonight. Her sister Vaughn was the only family she had left now. It never bothered her before, but her sister needed her now more than ever, and Bexley had begun to resent the distance that separated them. *It won't after tomorrow*, she reminded herself. *Tomorrow you will kiss all of this goodbye and head for the Big Apple.*

Bexley swallowed the lump in her throat and sprinted through the surf, not caring that the bottom edges of her skirt were getting splashed by the water kicking up in her wake. She turned to watch as her friends made their way more carefully through the gentle surf toward her. So different they all were. Yet, somehow, they'd gelled. Made connections Bexley had never let herself have before. Yes, she would miss her friends. More than she would ever admit to anyone. Even them.

chapter Two

Kai paced josh's living room, scrolling through the songs on his cousin's phone, which was hooked up to the home's sound system. The bluesy guitar riff of Laguna's own John Heussenstamn Trio filled the space, making Kai smile as he played along in this mind. His fingers twitched in the air and his eyes closed, lost in the sound that filled the open and airy space around him.

"Eh-hem," Josh coughed out from across the room, causing Kai's eyes to fly open.

"Cuz! It's about time. You almost ready?" Kai crossed the room and gave Josh an enthusiastic man-hug—shaking hands clasped, left hand patting the back while leaning in toward each other. But not *too* close. "Thanks for having me down, man. It's been a slow summer for guitar lessons. Have way too much time on my hands. And I can't wait to meet sweet little Francie," he said, picking up a framed picture of the toddler. "She's adorable. Has the family dimple, I see."

"She sure does," Josh said, looking affectionately at his daughter's picture. "We're so glad you're here. Sorry about the work thing. Just had to get some final paperwork on a deal out the door. Hey, I can't wait for you to see Holls—" Josh cleared his throat. "Not sure if I mentioned it or not, but she actually goes by her real first name now that she's off-air. Madison. I still can't help but call her Holly sometimes," Josh said, a smitten look crossing his handsome features. "She doesn't mind it when we're alone, though," he whispered, and winked.

Kai laughed, running a hand through his dark brown hair; if you asked the ladies, they might call it black. His ice blue eyes lit with amusement at his cousin's comment. He remembered Holly well from high school, but it had been a long time since he'd seen her. He'd always felt bad about the way Josh had handled things on-air with his fake shomance Laura, and the betrayal of his high school sweet heart—Holly. But Josh had redeemed himself, and if Holly forgave him, Kai certainly could. They were blood afterall.

"What's happening in this big city of yours tonight?" Kai asked, taking in the expensive new flat screen mounted over the double-sided stone fireplace that joined the cozy living space with the dining area. He was happy for this new success for his cousin. He never thought he'd say it, but Josh was a damn fine investment manager. And apparently, judging by the new high-end touches around the living room, he was good at his job.

It had just been a shock to Kai when he first found out Josh was giving up his dreams of acting and going into the financial business with his father. No one had wanted to succeed at being an actor more than Josh. He'd been so driven in high school it had almost cost him everything. He was damn lucky that Holly—*man, that's gonna take some getting used to*—Madison was able to forgive him and open her heart again. There was no way Kai would ever let a job come between himself and true love. It's why he hadn't gone into the family business. He'd seen firsthand how being married to your work could break apart a family.

But he wasn't worried about his cousin. What Josh and Madison had was as true as it got. Kai shook his head. He'd give just about anything to have what they shared. To find true love and put it above all else—unlike his parents.

Someday, Kai told himself.

"Well, you know we have the annual fireworks at Heisler Park. But I think this year we're watching them from some spot the girls have staked claim on. The park's more family friendly, but we're going to a goodbye party for one of our friends. So, I'm just going where I'm told," Josh said and laughed.

"Smart man," Kai said, gathering up his car keys. "I thought maybe I'd drive. That way, if you want to drive home with Madison you can. Or, I can be your DD tonight."

"Thanks, cuz!" he said, slapping Kai on the back. "Why don't we take my new ride, though, and you can bring it back for me later?"

Josh called out over his shoulder to Francie's nanny, who was sitting quietly in the kitchen with a mug of tea and a Melissa Foster romance novel. "Christina, we're heading out. We won't be too late, I don't think," he added. "Who knows? Madison's friend Bexley can be a little firecracker, sometimes," Josh admitted to Kai on their way out of the house.

It was a quick drive over to the beach bar where they were meeting Madison and her friends, but they needed to stop by Annie's house first to pick up her husband Hank. Kai remembered Annie well enough from high school, but it had been many years since he'd seen her, and he'd only met Hank once. Kai watched as he tried to escape through his front door, three kids hanging on to him in various stages of goodbye. Hank handed the baby to a teenager who scooped her up and had her laughing before he even made it to the car.

Hank hadn't changed much since the first time they'd met. Same red hair. Except maybe he sported a slight dad body now. "Hey, Hank! Long time," Kai said as Hank slid in the back seat of

Josh's Maserati Levante. Kai ran his hands over the deep maroon leather of the SUV's interior. Sure beat the cracked, sun-faded interior of his beater Jeep. Then again, he lived on a teacher's salary, much to his father's and uncle's chagrin. They still tried to recruit him, no matter how many times he said no and despite the fact that it would be such a colossal mismatch. Kai lived and breathed music, not numbers.

They got to the beach late, as Kai suspected they would. Laguna might be a little town, but it drew a nice crowd on the Fourth. They made their way through the sand to a small walk-up style bar that looked as if it might've been erected for just one night, it was so janky. It had a huge open-air porch, though, with a million-dollar view of the Pacific, so Kai wasn't complaining.

"What do you guys want to drink?" Josh asked. "My treat, to celebrate the new deal that just went through."

As Josh pushed his way to the bar, getting stopped frequently by girls asking for a picture, Kai and Hank hung out on the patio, leaning against a tall two-top table.

"So, what have you been up to?" Hank asked Kai. "I haven't seen you in ages."

"Yeah, I had to get out of here. I went up to LA for a while and tried the music scene, but it wasn't my thing. As much as I love music, I hate big cities and all the crap that comes with them. Threw me off track for a couple years, but I finally figured my shit out. Went to college, got my degree, and now I teach middle schoolers how to slay their instruments instead."

Hank was laughing as Josh came back and handed them their drinks. Kai took a healthy swallow of his Coke. "Cheers, Josh. Congrats on landing another big deal."

"Thanks, man. Working for my dad is something I never thought I'd see happen, but when I really got into it, I discovered I loved it. And I'm actually a natural at it—unlike acting," he admitted, cringing.

A pretty girl with bleached blond hair pulled high into a messy bun came bouncing up to the table, her perky breasts doing more of the bouncing than anything else. "Oh my gosh, you're Josh from *Laguna Nights*, right?" She squealed and waved two other friends over. "Will you sign our shirts?" She reached in her purse and dug out a Sharpie, handing it to Josh before he could answer.

Kai watched as Josh's demeanor shifted and his actor's smile slid onto his face. He flashed a grin at the girls and they all seemed to swoon. *Oh, brother.* Kai looked over at Hank, who rolled his eyes in response. "Does this happen all the time still?" Kai asked.

"Nah, man. Most people here have gotten used to having him back in town, and him and Madison being together. They're regular locals now like everyone else. But the holidays bring in tourists, and that's when recognition and excitement seem to pick back up again." Hank took a big swig of his Asylum ale and cringed.

Josh was in mid-signature, his hand resting on the girl's back, when Kai felt arms wrap around him from behind. "So this is what you boys get up to while we aren't around?"

Kai spun around and saw Madison there, grinning at him with her pretty blue eyes. He held on to her hands and pulled back, taking her in. "Wow! Holly—I mean, Madison! It's been way too long. Look at you. You look stunning as usual," he said and kissed her affectionately on the cheek. "Motherhood becomes you."

Madison blushed prettily as Josh finished signing the last girl's shirt and managed to disentangle himself from their attention. Man, Kai would not want that kind of recognition or imposition in his life. He was grateful he hadn't gotten pulled into the whole *Laguna Nights* drama, and had managed to stay off all but one episode.

Madison brushed past Kai to stand next to Josh, wrapping her arms around his waist and kissing him as if they were still in high school. *Lucky bastard.*

"Aw, man. Get a room, you two," he heard. He swiveled his head and came face to face with the most gorgeous woman he'd ever seen. Her dark auburn hair hung long and thick around her face, which was kissed with a smattering of freckles across the tops of her cheeks. "Take a picture, it lasts longer," she said to Kai, who was still staring at her like a speechless fool.

"Can I?" he asked, half joking. She shrugged, as if used to this sort of thing.

Kai pulled out his phone and snapped an up-close picture of the woman, her green eyes pulling to him even from behind the lens. *No, green isn't quite right. There's gold in there too*, he mused.

"Want a name for that face, or are you gonna turn into some weird, creepy stalker dude?" Bexley asked, then stopped, stricken, when she heard Annie's gasp from behind her. "I'm sorry, Annie. I didn't mean it like that."

Kai looked around the group, confused about what was happening. Luckily, Madison stepped in and smoothed over the awkwardness. "Kai, you remember Annie from high school, of course, and this is my new friend Bexley. She works—crap! I mean, she worked at the resort with me. Unfortunately, she's leaving Laguna Beach tomorrow for a new job opportunity," she said, her voice sounding genuinely sad. "Bex, this handsome devil is Josh's cousin, Kai Donovan."

Bexley. What kind of name is that? Kai wondered as he looked at the woman who just slammed into his world and tipped it upside down.

She slid a hand toward Kai and said, "Bexley Rue, the one and only."

chapter Three

Bexley lifted her brow when Josh's cousin Kai took her hand in his, turned it over, and kissed the back of it softly, his eyes never leaving hers.

Kai.

Hmm . . . he was certainly an unexpected perk to her night, not that she needed one.

"Well, aren't you just a charmer," she said, her green eyes lit with amusement.

"Bexley Rue, is it? What an unusual name."

Bex smiled, pleased. Her father, a poet, had gifted her with it. Her mother, ever more practical, had given her sister a family name. "Thanks. My father named me. He believed in fairies and all things magical, so he wanted me to have a name that matched."

The corner of Kai's mouth lifted into a delicious half-grin that brought light to his clear blue eyes, more like the color of finely cut aquamarines, Bex's birthstone. *Like the sea*.

"It matches perfectly. So, Bexley, this is your going away party? That's unfortunate."

Bexley saw the sly smile on Annie's face as if saying, *Mm-hmm. Told you so*.

Madison beat her to the punch. "Yeah, we're going to miss her terribly. Still haven't been able to find anyone qualified enough to replace her."

"Oh, and what is it you do, Miss Rue?" Kai asked, his eyes sweeping her face with interest. She couldn't help but notice the adorable dimple that lit up his left cheek when he grinned. She almost, for just a minute, regretted that she was leaving the next day.

"I was a massage therapist for the spa at the Mondrian, but I have a communications degree from Sac state. My sister needs some help with a new business she launched last year that's taking off way faster than she imagined, so I'm gonna be putting those business skills back to work in the Big Apple."

"Wow. You really are a puzzle, aren't you? All full of surprises. Well, can we make a toast then?"

Everyone lifted their glasses, and looked at Kai to see what he would say. "Here's to Bexley. May the road she travels upon next be the one that leads her home. Cheers!"

Bexley gulped, her eyes never leaving Kai's. *Oh, sweet baby Jesus.* She would be in so much trouble with this one if she were staying. She finished off her beer and looked around the table at her friends. This was the closest she'd come to having a tribe of "her people" in a long, long time. And now she was leaving. She got a little choked up. "Can we grab a fresh round of drinks and head out to the beach? I'd really like to see the last set of Laguna fireworks from the shore before I leave. I'm really gonna miss you guys."

Josh smiled at her and grinned. "We'll miss you, too, Bex. Who's gonna walk over and make me banana pancakes on Saturday mornings?" he asked with a grin. Bexley had been living in the small cottage behind Josh and Madison's home for the past six months now.

"I left the recipe with Madison. The secret is in the vanilla."

Madison laughed. "That, and the fresh organic bananas she buys at the farmers' market. I'm not promising that they'll taste anything like Bexley's, just for the record."

"Hey, why don't Hank and I go grab a fresh round, and you guys go find a spot on the beach? Just text me where you are, babe," Josh said to Madison. He kissed her on the cheek before making his way back inside to the little shack's bar.

Kai tossed a twenty onto the table and led the way out of the bar and onto the sand, the band still playing its steel drum and bodies still pressed against one another to the seductively slow rhythm of the reggae sound it was making. Kai stopped for a moment on the outskirts of the crowd and just listened, his head nodding in time with the music.

"Madison tells me you're a music teacher," Bexley said to Kai as Madison and Annie swayed to the music beside them.

"I am," Kai said, a smile lighting his face. "I love music. It's my life. Any time there's music playing, I'm a happy man."

"You sound easy enough to please," she said with a sly grin.

"I'm a simple man these days. I used to live in LA, and the scene there just wasn't my vibe."

Bexley looked out of the corner of her eyes at Kai as he got lost in the music for a moment, watched as his hands mimicked the beat of the drums.

"Do you play other instruments, as well?"

"Yeah. I can play pretty much anything, though after the guitar, piano and drums are my favorite."

Wow. That's hot. For some reason, an image of Kai in a pair of dark jeans and nothing else, sitting at a piano and playing something just for her washed over her, and the sexiness of it went straight to her belly. Her mouth was suddenly dry and she wished that Josh would hurry the hell up with those drinks.

"Do you play anything?" Kai asked in return.

Bex looked up just as his eyes finished grazing over her body, catching him in the act. He grinned, that dimple of his screaming out to her to *look at me!* Oh, she'd noticed all right. More than she should have. *You are leaving tomorrow, girlfriend. Reel in those hormones!*

"I don't," she said, sounding wistful.

"Come on, you two. Let's go find a place to plant our butts before the prime real estate is gone," Madison called out.

Bexley continued her thought as they followed behind their friends, who had slyly walked ahead. "We moved around a lot when I was growing up. Never really settled anywhere long enough for me to take lessons. I think we moved to a new place practically every year."

"Oh, was one of your parents in the military?" Kai asked.

It was a fair question. "No. My dad just had a wanderer's soul. He couldn't stay put for very long. He was a poet, and was constantly seeking new inspiration and scenery. It made for an interesting life."

"Did he earn his living writing, or was that just a hobby?" he asked thoughtfully.

Bex looked up at Kai, who was a good six inches taller than she was. Even in the dark, those eyes shone out at her like beacons. He was looking directly into her eyes and they paused for a moment, staring at each other, but neither saying a word. The heat and attraction Bex felt was instant and raw. The fluttery feeling in her stomach usually didn't come this quickly. *Or last very long*, she reminded herself.

She cleared her throat, trying to think of only happy thoughts tonight. Like the roar of the ocean ahead of her, and the sound of her two closest friends laughing. The crunchy feel of the sand as she shuffled her feet through it, long ago forgetting where she'd left her sandals. She looked up at Kai, noticing the way his dark hair flipped up a little as it hit his ears, and how strong his jawline looked as it angled toward her. His lips were full and wide, and she had to drag her eyes away, lest she start thinking too much about how they would taste.

"Uh, where were we?" she asked, momentarily forgetting what they were talking about.

"Your dad," he said, grinning at her, well aware of his affect on her.

Damn! She nodded. "Oh, yeah. He was a writer. Travel magazines mostly, though he wrote and published a lot of poetry too. He was pulling together a collection for a book he was working on when he passed away."

"I'm so sorry to hear that. I didn't realize he was gone," Kai said, reaching a hand out and placing it on her arm. "We don't have to talk about this."

"No, it's okay. It's been so long that I'm kind of used to him being gone now," she said and shrugged.

"Are you really? I lost my mother five years ago. Drunk driver.

There's not a day that goes by that I don't miss the hell out of her," Kai admitted. "Time goes on, but the absence the heart feels never really lessens, does it?"

Bexley was stunned. She hadn't met many guys who would talk so freely to her about such personal topics. Usually guys were all sports, finances, and themselves. Rarely did they seem interested enough to dig so deeply about her, especially so early on.

"I—" Bexley started.

"How about right here?" Madison asked, turning to face Bexley and Kai.

It took everything in Bexley to pull her eyes away from Kai's in that moment. The magnetic pull between them felt palatable to her. *This is crazy!*

"I—it's fine with me," Bex said, at an unusual loss of words. "Kai, you cool with this?"

Kai grinned, nodding. "I'm down. I'm just along for the ride. This is your night," he said.

Bexley couldn't help but grin back at him. He was so easygoing and fun to be around. There was just something about him that put her at ease.

Bexley plopped down into the sand, tucking her short skirt around her legs and stretching them out long in front of her. She looked up and saw Madison texting Josh their whereabouts. Should be easy enough, they were pretty close to the shoreline.

The beach was crowded tonight, but nothing out of the norm for the Fourth of July.

"So, Madison, how has life been treating you since the *Reality TV Triple Play* show aired? That kind of took me by surprise when Josh told me about it," Kai said, settling down next to Bexley on the sand and wiping his hands off on his shorts.

"Yeah, it took us by surprise, too, the way it all went down. But, honestly, it felt like good closure, and now Francie has her college all paid for. So it worked out well in the end."

"That's great! I actually watched some of it, and was just so happy for Josh that you'd come back into his life. Kinda sucks the way they manipulated the situation, but you're the best thing that ever happened to him. Whatever it took to get you guys back together, I'm glad it happened."

"Me too, cuz," Josh said from above him. He juggled the drinks in his hands, handing Kai a cold can of Coke and giving Bexley another Una Mas.

Annie stood and grabbed the blanket Hank had been carrying tucked under his arm. He passed off a couple of bottles of waters to Madison. "Thanks, babe," Annie said, helping Hank spread the large blanket onto the beach as well as they could with people still walking by.

Annie, Hank, Madison, and Josh settled onto the blanket and patted it, indicating that Bex and Kai should come join them. Kai looked over at Bexley with a question in his eyes, and Bex looked back over at Josh and answered, "Nah, I think we're good. Thanks though."

Bexley didn't mind a little sand, and she was quite comfortable where she was for once in her life.

chapter Four

The yawns came quickly after the fireworks, Kai noticed. First came Annie's, then Madison's. He was too energized after talking to Bexley the whole time. He was more interested in the way her face lit up than the way the sky did. It had nothing on Bexley Rue.

The fireworks paled in comparison to the way Bexley's eyes came to life and crinkled at the corners from laughter. The way her nose scrunched up, crowding her freckles under her lashes. Or the way those lush lips parted and sighed when she was completely consumed by the beauty of the crowd and scene around her.

Kai had never been so instantly taken by a woman before; but he knew one thing after spending just a few short hours with her:

he didn't want the night to end. He needed more of Bexley, and time was running out.

"Where to now?" she asked, standing up and twisting her hips to shake the excess sand from her skirt and legs. She laughed and kicked her legs out several times like a wet puppy.

"Here, let me help," said Kai, still sitting. He rose to his knees and reached his hand out to brush the sand that was stuck to her legs. He held his breath as his fingers trailed the fine muscles of her calves. Her skin was so damn smooth.

He cleared his throat and stood. "Better?" he asked, his eyes trained on hers.

A smirk rode those full lips of hers. "Much. So . . . who's up for a little more fun tonight?" Bexley asked her group of friends. She looked at her phone. "Guys, it's not even eleven," she said with obvious excitement.

Annie was the first to graciously back out. "I'm so sorry, Bex. We only had our sitter for a few hours, and the kids get up so early. We really need to call it a night." She wrapped her arms around her friend, giving her a quick hug. "I promise we'll get out to New York sometime really soon. I'll miss our coffee chats and power walks, Bex."

A sadness washed over Bexley's gorgeous green eyes, dulling them. Kai wanted to bring back the sparkle that was there only a few moments ago when they were all talking and laughing during the fireworks display. He'd do anything to bring that smile back before the night ended. And Kai was not about to let it end this soon.

Hank finished folding their blanket back up and gave Bexley a hug goodbye. "Stay safe, kiddo. Okay? New York is a bigger pond than Laguna. Carry something to protect yourself, and don't wander around at night. If someone comes at you, go for their eyes or throat."

"Nice, Hank," laughed Madison.

"What? It's true," insisted Hank.

Bexley nodded, but the light still didn't reach back up to her eyes. "Yes, Dad," she mocked, giving Hank a sincere hug. "Kiss those babies of yours goodbye for me. I'm gonna miss them."

After Annie and Hank strolled off through the sand, Bexley smiled again and turned toward Josh and Madison. "Please tell me you guys are up for some fun. The night is still young!" Bexley grabbed Madison's hand, her eyes pleading. "It's my last night. Come on. We must do something epic!"

Madison laughed. "Girl, I have a toddler at home. My epic nights are long over," she admitted. "Francie has been having night terrors lately, and I want to be there if she has any tonight. Especially with the fireworks. I hope she was even able to sleep through them." She hugged Bexley for a long time. "Besides, I'll see you tomorrow afternoon when I drive you to the airport. Three-ish, right?"

Bex nodded, but her shoulders sagged.

"Hey, I'm up for hanging out a little bit more tonight if you are," Kai said, looking at Bexley. "I'm only in town for a few days, and this might be my only chance to see Laguna at night, since I'm staying with these two snoozers," Kai joked as he nodded toward Josh and Madison.

"Yeah, never thought I'd be happy to call it a night at eleven o'clock, but kids seem to change everything. Francie calls the shots at our house these days," Josh said, laughing. "But that's actually a great idea, Kai. I'll drive home with Madison, and why don't you keep my car and bring Bex home later? That'll work out perfectly, if you're okay with it, Bexley."

Bexley seemed to think about it for a moment, then turned to Kai, her energy suddenly returning. "Only if you're willing to do whatever I ask tonight. I am dying for an epic last night in Laguna Beach to remember over all others." She lifted a brow and gave Kai a piercing look. "You in?"

Madison and Josh laughed, and Josh placed a hand on Kai's shoulder. "Man, you are in trouble, cuz. Better you than me. Keep her in a semi-straight line tonight, will ya? And don't let her do anything to get arrested," he half joked.

Bex swatted Josh's arm. "Hey! I resemble that remark," she said and scowled playfully. "I promise I won't do anything to get Kai arrested."

"Well, that's a relief," Madison teased. "Please, no phone calls waking us up in the middle of the night to bail you out, Bex. Love you, girl," she said, hugging her friend good night.

They watched Josh and Madison make their way back up the beach with the other firework-goers who were heading toward their cars to try to beat traffic home. Kai turned to Bexley and grinned.

"Finally, I have you all to myself," he said and laughed, raking his hand through his thick, wavy hair. "So, what does the lady of honor want to do first?"

"A shot?" Bexley grinned mischievously, a single dimple popping out. "Come on. Jorge makes the best Fireball shooters on the beach," she said, taking his hand and dragging him across the sand back to LagunaMatata. Kai didn't think it was the right time to tell Bexley that he didn't drink, but knew he'd have to fess up before too long.

He loved the way her hand felt in his as they walked across the beach. It was small and warm, comforting in his own.

"So, Miss Rue, tell me a little more about yourself. If I'm endangering my good reputation on a wild night in Laguna with you, the least I deserve is a little more background on my future cellmate."

She turned her head and gave Kai a pointed look. "Very funny. Are you a comedian as well as a school teacher then?"

"Seriously, tell me what makes Bexley, well . . . Bexley."

Bexley didn't even know where to start. "Shots first, twenty questions later," she conceded. "I need a little fire in my belly if I'm about to spill my life story to a stranger. Even if he is a handsome one."

Kai swallowed hard. She was flirting with him all right. *Damn.* He didn't know where the night was taking them, and they had absolutely no chance of a future together, but hell if he would waste it with doubts and what-ifs. He was going to enjoy this night at any cost to his heart.

"Jorge," Bexley called when they saddled up to the rickety wooden bar, "Fireball shots, pronto!"

Jorge swung a towel over his shoulder and smiled at Bex from the other end of the bar where he stood with two beautiful blondes who were clearly making eyes at him, despite his casual indifference. "Sexy Bexy!" he called out when he spotted her. "Coming right up for you, my friend."

The two blondes shot daggers their way after Jorge's sudden shift in attention toward Bexley. Kai wasn't really thrilled either, quite frankly, though he had no right to feel jealous. "Sexy Bexy?" he mumbled under his breath at her.

She elbowed him and whispered back, "Shut up," trying not to laugh.

Jorge strolled down to where they stood at the bar and set down two colorful "Drunk 1" and "Drunk 2" shot glasses. He eyed Kai up and down. "Who's your new friend, señorita?"

"Behave, Jorge," Bexley said and laughed. She placed a twenty on the bar and slid the shots toward them. "This is my new friend

Kai. He's Josh's cousin, so play nice."

A smile broke out across Jorge's wide, stern face. "Well, why didn't you say so? Josh is a good friend of mine and is helping me get some small jobs on set with his producer friends. Right now I'm really just a gofer, but I'm hoping to work my way up to assistant to the director some day," he confided.

"Good for you," Kai said sincerely. "It's a rough business to get into, but you seem like you have a plan. Stick with it, and you'll go far."

"Hmmph," was all Bexley said, before lifting her shot and facing Kai. "Sticking's not my thing, but taking this shot is. Bottom's up, Kai."

She lifted the shot to her mouth and Kai watched as the amber liquid swirled down the glass and over her full lips. It was as if the shot emptied in slow motion and he couldn't take his eyes off her mouth. When she was done she hollered, "Woo! Hit me again, Jorge."

She hadn't noticed that Jorge was off pouring a Guinness for another customer. Kai still couldn't take his eyes from her lips and wondered briefly what the Fireball would taste like on her. Though he wasn't a drinker anymore, he sure wouldn't pass up the chance to lick the traces of it from her mouth; he knew it would burn its way down his throat and punch him in the gut, just like this raw lust was doing right now.

"Here, finish mine," Kai said, sliding his shot over to Bexley.

"Why didn't you drink it? You were supposed to throw it back with me, old man," she teased. "Speaking of which, just how old are you anyway?" she asked, cocking a perfectly arched brow in his direction.

"Geez, woman. How old do you think I am?" Kai asked, dancing around the first part of her question.

She slit her eyes and brought her finger to her mouth, teasing him once again with those damn lips. She bit her finger in contemplation and Kai nearly lost it, having to stuff his hands in his short's pockets to keep from grabbing the back of her head and all that gorgeous red hair and devouring her lips with his own.

"Thirty-two?" she guessed.

"Close. Thirty-four."

"Almost nailed it," she said and shrugged. "Still, older men are so sexy," she said, winking. "All stable and shit."

"I'll show you stable," he said, half in jest. He leaned forward and closed the space between them. Not the setting he normally wanted a first kiss to take place with a girl, but she was so damn feisty. He just wanted to prove to her that he wasn't old and lame just because he didn't do shots and had a few years on her. Older didn't mean boring. It meant confident in Kai's eyes. And he damn well knew that when he kissed her, there was no going back. He was going to claim that sexy little mouth of hers and make her beg for more kisses later.

His mouth found hers easily, though he teased her with his lips first. He made her wait. He noticed that she'd shut her eyes and was ready for his mouth to meet hers. He leaned in and brushed his lips slowly over hers once, then twice, their anticipated breaths mingling together in the warm night air.

"Bex," he said, sliding one hand behind her head and up into her thick mass of hair. He grasped a handful, not too hard, but to navigate her closer to his mouth again. "God, I want to taste you so bad right now, but not here," he whispered. "You're better than a throwaway kiss in a bar. Let's go somewhere else."

"I know just the place," she whispered into his ear, her lips brushing it in the process.

The surge of heat went straight between his legs as he imagined those lips clasping his ear, her tongue drawing the line of it, trailing down his jaw. God, he wanted to taste that tongue completely, wrap his own around hers and draw it in. His hands left her hair and traveled down her arms, resting on her hips. He drew her in to his body and they were mere inches apart.

"When this kiss happens, I guarantee it'll be one worth remembering after you leave Laguna," he growled, their bodies nearly pressing together.

"I'm counting on it," she said, then threw back the remaining shot. She pushed off against him and, swaying her hips, led them out of the bar and back into the balmy night air.

chapter Five

Oh my god, screamed Bexley inside her head. That teasing, that brushing of Kai's lips against her own, had nearly unhinged her. Now all she could think about was grabbing him by his thick, full hair and taking his mouth for a test-drive. This was not good, not good at all. And yet . . .

Kai had walked into her life tonight for a reason.

Even if it was just one night, Bexley decided then and there to make it the most memorable one in history. She grabbed Kai's hand as they pushed through the crowd in front of the bar. A small group was still swaying to the beat of the band, but the steel drums were gone and softer notes floated on the air in rhythm to the ebb and flow of the water's tide.

Kai tugged Bexley's hand, spinning her back toward him. She came chest to chest with him, caught off guard by the sudden movement it created. She rested her hands on his shirt and looked up at him. *Why, oh why, does he have to be so darn handsome*, thought Bexley as she peered into his bright blue eyes. Those eyes suddenly looked predatory as they held her own, never once breaking the spell as Kai's hands went to her hips and he began moving against her to the rhythm of the band.

Bexley swayed her hips against his, the contact nearly driving her insane. The night air was cooling off and a light coastal breeze brushed over them, making Bexley's arms pebble. Kai ran his warm palms over her skin, taking her hands in his as they still swayed in sync to the bluesy tones that now filled the bar area. Bexley closed her eyes. *Oh, yes. I could get used to this.*

She felt Kai's lips brush her neck as she gripped his hips. The hardness of his hip bone, as it moved in time with her own, shots spears of white hot heat straight between Bexley's legs this time. She snaked her hand up his chest and around his neck, wanting so badly to draw his mouth to hers.

"Uh-uh-uh," Kai whispered in her ear as he ground his hips against her even closer. He was just as turned on as she was, but he said, "When I kiss you for the first time—and I mean, really kiss you—I don't want an audience, Bexley. I want to feel you under my hands and taste you between my lips, and I want some privacy when I do. Because I could do some naughty, naughty things with that mouth of yours, and I want you all to myself when I do."

Bexley was caught off guard by his candor, but now all she could think about was what he wanted to do with her mouth. "Follow me," she said.

They held hands and parted the crowd, walking away from the partygoers as they strolled down the beach toward her favorite spot.

"Where are we going?" Kai asked.

"My favorite cove. It's just around the corner, but there's privacy. Madison, Annie, and I actually came down here earlier tonight. But I feel like I want to show it to you, too, before the night is over. I'm not sure why, but I think you'll love it just as much as we do."

They walked under the moonlight in companionable silence. Bexley loved the feel of Kai's hand in her own. It was so big and masculine. She immediately thought of how good they would feel over her skin, massaging the tight muscles in her shoulders, easing away her worries over moving. She hadn't had many before tonight, but now she suddenly had doubts swarming through her mind. Was she doing the right thing? Would there be men like Kai in New York City? Could she handle an office job again? She'd had one during the first year after college as she worked her way through massage therapy school, and she was glad when she'd become certified and could leave the rat race for good . . . or so she thought.

"You okay in there?" Kai asked, stopping as they neared the cove. "You suddenly feel really tense. What's going on in that mind of yours?"

Bexley stopped and looked up at Kai. "Honestly? I was thinking about having your hands all over me," she said coyly, trying to shake the nerves and change the subject.

"That wasn't the vibe I was getting, Bex. Here, let's sit down and talk," he said, pulling her hand in his own and easing her in front of him on the sand. Bexley sat looking out at the ocean, her back against Kai's chest. This felt so good, so natural. *Why now?*

She leaned her head back fully against his chest and closed her eyes, taking in a deep lungful of the crisp, cool evening air. The temperature had dropped nicely, and the evening was a perfect reminder of the warm summer nights Laguna had.

"Hey," Kai said, pulling Bexley's hair off of one of her shoulders and exposing her neck. He leaned down and brushed his lips over her clavicle bone. "What has you so stressed? I thought this was going to be a happy night. An epic night."

She sighed, melting into him. "It is. I just started overthinking the move all of a sudden and questioning if this was the right thing for me to do."

"Where's the hesitancy coming from?" Kai asked, running his fingers along her arm as they sat facing the ocean.

Bexley could feel the in and out of Kai's breath and had to reel herself back in to focus on the conversation and not his lips again. It would be so easy to totally surrender to him tonight and never look back. But Bexley was afraid if she got too much of a taste for Kai, it might not be so easy to keep her promise to her sister and leave for New York the next day.

"Do you really want to hear all of this?" Bexley asked, half joking.

"If it's on your mind and is important to you, then yes, I want to hear it," Kai said.

Bexley couldn't remember the last time she'd felt so torn between being turned on like crazy and wanting to actually have a deeper conversation with a man. It had been a long time since she'd let someone in enough to worry about such things. It was easier to move on to the next thing if there wasn't anything holding her back. So Bexley often kept the strings loose and the feelings at surface level; but Kai was having none of that, and it was kind of hot.

"Well," she said, taking a deep breath, "I've been doing massage therapy for almost six years now, and I love it. I knew it wouldn't be a forever career, but I thought about opening my own spa or wellness center one day, rather than leaving the field entirely. I loved working with Madison, and she was helping me learn the business side of running a spa, too."

"That's an amazing idea. Why don't you do that?"

"Because that takes capital I just don't have right now. And because my sister needs my help."

"Isn't there anyone else she could hire? I mean, no offense, I'm sure you're the best for the job, but does she know about your passion to own your own business?"

"No, she doesn't. If she did, I know she would encourage me to follow my dreams. Vaughn is my older sister, my only sister. I told you that I'd lost my father, but I didn't mention that I lost my mother at the same time, too. After our parents died, she was all I had left. But instead of turning to her for support, I pulled away. She was out of college by then and working in New York. It was easy to let the physical distance be the reason for the emotional separation too. But, honestly, it was just easier to not *feel* so much anymore. My heart was so heavy after my mom and dad passed."

"Aw, man, Bexley." Kai wrapped his arms around her protectively, drawing her even closer. "May I ask how they passed? They seem awfully young for you to have lost them both."

"They were. It was a small plane accident. They were flying home from Washington state after a writer's retreat my dad had spoken at. Mom never usually went along, but she did this time. I guess there was a technical malfunction on the plane, and the pilot lost control. There were five people on board, and no one survived."

"Bex, my God, I'm so sorry," Kai said and kissed her temple. "They were too young to go. I hate that you're without them. It sounds like you were close."

"We were," Bexley said, staring up at the moon that was so clear in the night sky. "Especially with my father. I was a Daddy's girl, and I was the one who usually went on writer's retreats with him. I'd often set up my travel massage chair and take clients while traveling with him. It worked out nicely. But this time it was near my parents' anniversary, so they wanted to turn it into a celebration trip. My only solace is knowing that they had a wonderful, romantic time together before they passed. But I can't help feeling guilty that my mom was on board, when it should have been me," Bex said quietly.

Kai turned Bexley around so that she faced him. He held her shoulders in his hands and looked down into her eyes, intently. "Bex, it should not have been you on that plane, do you understand me? It shouldn't have happened to your parents either, but please, never ever think for a moment that it should have been you."

He brushed her hair from her face as tears threatened to slip from her eyes. She looked down at the sand to catch her breath.

"Bex," he whispered, lifting her chin so that her eyes met his. "I am so sorry for the losses in your life, but I'm glad you weren't on that plane."

She lost it then, tears spilling over onto her cheeks. "Why? It doesn't even matter. This is just one night, Kai," she said.

"Because then I would never have known this," he said, his

mouth coming down softly onto hers.

He took his time with her lips, tasting them, teasing them gently before he finally parted them with his tongue. When their mouths met fully, the heat searing between them even in the slow, sexy dance they were performing with their tongues, Bex wanted more. So much more. Her hands slipped up to grasp the hair behind his head. She moaned into Kai's mouth as he increased the depth and intensity of his kiss. His hands went up and cupped the sides of her face gently, a sharp contrast to the heat that was building between them.

"Kai," she said breathlessly as the kiss ended.

"Bex, this kiss was meant to happen. Me meeting you? This was meant to happen tonight. Please don't ever say you were supposed to be on that plane. I never want to imagine a life where that kiss hadn't just happened."

Bex laughed, the intensity of their intimacy fading as she snuggled against his chest. "It's just one night, Kai, but I'm glad my last night in Laguna is with you."

chapter Six

Kai held Bexley to his chest, confused about why feelings were rushing in so fast, and so protectively, for her. They'd just met a few hours ago, and suddenly Kai didn't want the night to end at all. He wanted to bring that smile back to Bexley's eyes, make her forget about the pain for a while. He cursed under his breath that they only had this one night before she moved across the damn country, but he was determined to make it the memorable night she longed to take with her.

"So, Miss Bexley Rue, what can I do to bring that smile back? You asked for an epic night, and I'm all yours," he said, tucking a stray hair behind her ear.

"Let's go swimming!" she said impulsively, the light returning. "I feel like I need a good dose of sea water to shake all these sad feelings. And I won't have a chance to swim again tomorrow, so it'll be my farewell to Laguna Beach." Bexley had already stood and was unzipping the side of her skirt before Kai could answer.

He stood slack jawed as she dropped her flouncy floral skirt to the sand. *This girl has no inhibitions.* Which Kai was entirely too happy to see. Bexley stood before him with nothing on but her black tank top and matching black panties.

Sweet mother of God, Kai whispered to himself. He was going to have a hard time not wanting more than a kiss from her before the night was through. Kai was a gentleman, but not a saint. And seeing Bexley turn and run toward the ocean, the black thong of her panties parting the soft skin of her behind, the muscles contracting in her cheeks with each stride . . . it was too much.

"You aren't going to make me swim alone are you?" she asked over her shoulder, a smile lighting her face under the moonlight.

He quickly lifted his black T-shirt over his head, leaving his shorts on since he was going commando underneath. He chased after Bexley toward the water, eliciting a squeal he found quite charming. He wanted to pull her down into the surf and kiss that sound right from her mouth. He longed for other things, too, but knew they weren't his to have, given their brief time together tonight. He feared he would be dreaming of Bexley's kisses for many months to come after she left.

He caught up to her just as she dove beneath the warm, salty water. He thought she was just going to wade in and splash around a little, but she'd fully submersed herself under the gentle waves. She broke the surface, her hair long and wet behind her, slick against the muscled shoulders of her back. Her ass was perfectly round and pert, and he wanted to wrap his mouth around hers and grab a handful of her sexy skin. Kai was harder than the rocks that lined the cove, and he was glad the water was up past his waist to hide just how sexy he found Bexley. He wondered if she had any idea how gorgeous she was.

She turned around to face him, wiggling a finger in his direction. He walked in farther until he met her in the water, now both in chest deep. She was the one to make the move this time, and when she did, it was all over for Kai. Passion was met with passion as their tongues swam back and forth. Kai's hands dropped to Bexley's small waist, and then slid down farther to cup her sweet ass. He grabbed a handful and yanked her closer to him, lifting her off the ocean floor as her legs wrapped around his waist. He felt her pubic bone pressing against him and deepened his kiss, taking more than he knew he had a right to. But he wanted Bexley more than he'd ever wanted anyone before. She was sweetness and she was fire, and he was totally drowning in her magic.

"Bexley," Kai groaned, "we need to stop." It took everything within him to pull back from the kiss and try to slow his heart and rushing testosterone. All he could think about was laying Bexley down in the sand and sliding deep inside of her. He wasn't that kind of guy, though, and he suddenly wanted to give Bexley more than that.

"What if I don't want to stop, Kai?" she said breathlessly against his cheek. She ran her tongue along his hard jawline and over to his ear, just as he'd fantasized about earlier in the night. She took in his earlobe and suckled, purring into his ear in the process. "What if I want to really live up my last night and make the most of this time together? What if I can't stop thinking about what's under these shorts and how I'd love to have your fingers inside of me?"

Kai sucked in a breath, turned on like crazy by her forwardness. "What if I don't want to just be a one-night stand for you, Bexley? What if I want more than that?" he countered.

"But what if I do?" she teased. "What if I want all of you before I leave, but can't give you more of me after I'm gone?"

He was at war with himself. He now wanted so much more than one night with Bexley, but she was in his ear and on his skin, and he could not tear himself away as she kissed her way into his heart.

He would give her whatever she wanted this one night, but he had no intention of letting her go from his life for good. This time as he covered her mouth again with his own, he held nothing back. Somehow, he would find a way for there to be more than just one night with Bexley—even if she wasn't able to see the possibility of it yet.

He was lost in her.

Kai loved the way she tasted of summer and cinnamon, and he longed to taste every inch of her. He lowered her into the water so they both stood pressed together, their mouths never separating. She pulled his lower lip into her mouth and sucked, biting it ever so lightly, and Kai felt a tugging that went straight to his loins.

He started to bring his hand up to her hair when she caught it in her own, her eyes trained on his. She took one of his fingers and slid it slowly, deeply into that sweet mouth of hers. She suckled his finger, riding it with her lips while she fucked him with her eyes. It was more than he could bear. He needed to feel her. He slid his other hand down her waist and under the hem of her panties. He was betting they'd be wet even if they hadn't been in the ocean. Kai traced along the sweet folds of her skin before sliding one of his fingers deep inside her. Bexley gasped as he pushed it all the way in. She sucked harder on his finger, moaning against it as he quickened his pace with his hand below the water's surface.

Kai pulled his finger from her mouth and brought his hand to the back of her head, pulling lightly on her hair to bring her mouth back to his. He inserted a second finger deep within her as their kiss deepened, her hips moving in time with the steady rhythm of his hand. When he curled his fingers and angled for her sweet spot, Bexley moaned against his mouth letting Kai know he was close. That she was close.

"Come for me, Bex," he whispered. "I want to feel you tighten around my fingers and release for me."

"Oh God, yes," Bexley cried, her breathing hitched and coming in pants as he moved faster. Even as the salt water cupped his hand as it rode against her body, he could feel how slippery and wet she was inside. Yeah, she was a little firecracker, all right. Such an unexpected surprise to his night. He wanted to watch her explode, lighting up his heart as if it were the sky.

She closed her eyes and pressed into his hand over and over again, rocking against him in rhythm to the gentle waves around them. The erotic back and forth had Kai so hard he was worried he'd release himself before she did, and he wasn't even trying to.

"Oh God, Kai," she called out. He loved hearing his name come from her lips as she climaxed around his fingers in the water. Her body shook from the intensity of the orgasm that ripped through her, and she fell against him, her arms wrapping around his neck as she came down, breath by breath. "Holy shit. Now that . . . that was epic." She laughed and then kissed him again. "Where in the world did you ever come from? And why couldn't we have met before my last night in Laguna?"

"Everything happens for a reason, Bex. Let's just make the

most of the time we've been given," Kai said. He was still wound tighter than strings on a new guitar, but he wanted to just hold her in the warm salty water, their bodies lightly swaying to the ocean's rhythm.

chapter *Seven*

They lay side by side on the sand after getting out of the ocean, holding hands across the void between them and looking up at the stars.

"There's a lot of unknown up there," Kai mused out loud.

Bexley turned onto her side and propped herself up on her elbow, looking over at Kai. "There's a lot of unknown down here too," she said, a half-smile taking over.

"There doesn't have to be," Kai said quietly.

"Hey," Bexley said, changing the subject, "I have an idea. Let's go wash up by the lifeguard stand and then I want to show you one of my favorite spots in Laguna. Are you still up for an adventure tonight?"

Kai smirked. "And what was that then?" he asked, nodding to the ocean where they'd just rocked each other's worlds. "That was about as adventurous as I've ever been before," Kai said and laughed.

Bexley smiled. "Okay, so I meant *another* adventure. Will you turn into a pumpkin if I don't get you home by midnight?"

Kai sat up and looked at Bexley. "I hate to break the news, but it's already past midnight." He stretched his arms out as if to inspect them. "Guess I'm good for a few more hours."

A look of mischief came over Bexley's face. "How about pulling an all-nighter with me then? I can sleep on the plane, and I'm having so much fun with you. What do you say to finding a bunch of sights to see around Laguna and making this a night neither of us will ever forget?"

Kai looked into Bexley's eyes as much as he could in the dark that separated them. He inched forward on the sand and cupped the back of Bexley's neck so they were only inches apart now. "Oh, I think you've already succeeded there," he admitted, closing the distance between them and kissing her. "You have no idea the effect you have on me, do you?"

"Thank you, Kai," Bexley said softly. "I know this has been the strangest night of meeting someone new for the first time. But I have loved getting to talk to you, and . . . well, you're an awfully good kisser," she teased.

"What else, Bex?" he breathed out slowly.

"Well," she drew out, "my body has never reacted quite this quickly or so intensely to someone before. I love the way you made my body hum to life, and—"

"And what, Bexley?" he growled, drawing her closer so they were nose to nose in the moonlight. "Tell me you feel this between us. Tell me this isn't all in my head. Because when I touched you, I saw stars. I wanted to take you, there, in the ocean. I wanted to surrender my heart to you, Bexley. I know you want to have just this one night, but I have to tell you something," Kai said, leaning in and biting her shoulder gently, then kissing the same spot with his warm lips. "You are going to be far too hard to chase out of my system after tonight if I already feel this way after a few hours. This thing that's happening between us? There's no distance that's going to be able to take this from us. Tell me you feel it too."

"Kai, I'm not built like you. I have a gypsy's heart and soul. This time I've been in Laguna . . . I've been here for a year, Kai. Other than going to college, it's the longest I've ever stayed in one place. I don't know how to stay, even if I wanted to. My sister, she really needs me right now. And, quite frankly, I need her too. Can we just enjoy each other's company and not push too hard about what comes next?"

Kai took a deep breath in and looked up at the stars. Bexley wished to God she could reach out and give him the comfort and reassurance he needed, but she knew it wouldn't be fair. She was leaving tomorrow, and that would be the end of this. She didn't want to go there in her mind yet, though. Selfishly, she wanted to spend as much time with him as possible, enjoying life and remembering how to be young, carefree, and uninhibited. Once she moved to New York, that would all change for her. And it wasn't a change she was entirely looking forward to. But it's one she would make for her sister's sake.

Kai stood, offering his hand to Bexley. "All right, Miss Rue. I'm all yours tonight. No strings attached. Just you, me, and a pocketful of stars to hang our worries on."

Bexley jumped up and joined Kai, grabbing his hand in hers. "Come on, then! We're wasting precious time."

She grabbed her skirt from the beach and sprinted off across the sand toward the outdoor showers closest to the lifeguard chair. Bexley got there first and was already rinsing off when Kai charged up, panting. "Where in the world did you learn to run like that, Bex?"

Bexley grinned, the warm water rinsing the sand from her curvy body. She wrung her skirt out under the light trickle of water, considering. "I'm used to moving around, Kai, remember?" she teased.

"I didn't know you meant literally!"

She stepped out from under the water and watched as Kai closed his eyes and ducked his head under the stream. She wished she could run her hands over his chest again, lick the running drops of water from the hard plains of his abs. And, dear God . . . she swallowed hard when she noticed the deep V of his hips that led her imagination straight to the center of his shorts. He had a light smattering of hair across his lower stomach where the cloth sagged slightly under the pressure of the running water. What she wouldn't give to run her fingers along that trail, to see how far down it went.

"Bex?" Kai said, interrupting her thoughts.

She chuckled guiltily, raking her eyes back up to his.

"You were thinking dirty thoughts again, weren't you, Miss Rue? Do I need to bend you over my knees and give you a good spanking?"

Laughter bordering on desire slipped from Bexley's mouth as she tried to form a coherent response. *Being spanked by Kai?* Her mouth went dry. She knew he was teasing, but the words formed images in her mind that she just couldn't erase. That she didn't want to erase.

"I think I could use a little discipline," she joked, walking toward him, hungry for another taste.

He splashed her with the spray. "If we don't stop this, we will never see the sights you want to show me, Bex. Behave yourself, wild cat."

She brushed up next to him, her firm breasts nearly grazing his chest as it rose and fell with her proximity. "I'm waiting on you, music man. Let's keep this party rolling," she said as she shimmied back into her wet skirt. She inhaled sharply when her eyes met Kai's again. There was so much heat and passion staring back at her. She wasn't sure whether to jump on him and start kissing the fuck out him, or run the other way.

Maybe her heart wasn't quite ready to play this close to fire.

He resolved the dilemma in her mind by closing the space between them. He wrapped one of his strong hands up under her wet hair and guided her mouth to his. Just before their lips met, he whispered, "You can't always run, Bex. Sometimes, you have to let yourself get caught."

His mouth crashed down on top of hers and demanded this time. Gone was the sweet first kiss on the beach and the sexy make-out session in the water. This. This was pure torture that shot heat straight between her legs and made her want to abandon her promises to her sister. Made her want to do the one thing she never did with men: let down the guard around her heart.

Their tongues worshipped each other as hands found skin. Kai's fingers trailed down her sides and found her waist again before quickly cupping her ass, hard, as he pulled her against his body. "I'm a patient man, Bexley. Do you feel this?" He pressed himself against her, her back arching over the small fence as she stared up into those intense blue eyes.

Oh, boy, did she ever feel that.

"You drive me insane. Never have I been so turned on so

quickly. That's not who I am. But you . . . you come strolling into my life, toss that sexy red hair my way, and get my blood boiling in six seconds flat." He backed up, raked a hand through his tousled dark hair. Bexley loved the way it looked at war with itself, just as Kai's emotions were struggling. "What am I going to do with you, Bexley?" he said, almost quietly.

"Accept me for who I am? Give me time? There's a lot you don't know yet—"

"Then tell me, damn it," he said, clearly getting frustrated.

"I will," Bexley whispered. "Can we go somewhere else first? I'd like to actually change out of these clothes and then take you to my favorite spot. We can chat easier there."

"Bex, I'd follow you just about anywhere right now. The ball's clearly in your court," he said, resting his forehead on hers. "I don't know what's happening to me right now, but I just know I like how I feel when I'm around you and I'm not ready for it to stop."

She wrapped her arms around him in a hug, her head resting flat against his chest. She listened to the steady beat of his heart and wished, for just the briefest moment, that things could be different. That she wasn't needed so desperately in New York. That she had a heart that could give and receive as easily as Kai seemed able to. That the very thought didn't make her want to run to New York even faster.

What the hell is wrong with me?

chapter Eight

They returned to Bexley's cottage behind Josh and Madison's house and snuck in to change. He'd grabbed his duffle bag from his Jeep and put on a fresh pair of khaki shorts and a new black T-shirt after a real shower. He was coming out of the bathroom when he caught a glimpse of Bexley in her room, her back to him.

He'd seen her nearly naked on the beach already, but seeing her like this, in her home with her T-shirt over her head about to slide down the long muscles of her back—it sucker-punched Kai in the gut. She was so beautiful it took his breath away. But it was more than that. She was fearless. It seemed so easy for her to pick up her life and move to the city, make a fresh start.

He'd been terrified to move to LA after high school; and then he'd hated every minute of it until he finally made the wise decision to go back to school. As soon as Kai graduated, he moved to Sonoma to be closer to his retired father and to teach middle school. It was the best decision he'd ever made. There, in the small town and open air, he could breathe. The quiet neighborhood streets, the town square. They all made him feel safe and at peace. The children were smart and eager to learn, and their parents had the finances to pay for private lessons, which helped supplement his meager teacher's income. He'd never be rich like his father and uncle were, but he had a life he loved.

Seeing Bexley standing there dressing in her room made him long for her in a way that surprised and saddened him. She wasn't his to imagine a future with. She was leaving later that day, since the new day had already snuck in on them while they were at the beach. And he wasn't sure what was worse: the fact that his time with her was running out, or knowing that even if she wasn't leaving, she wasn't really the settling down type.

She looked at him over her shoulder, a wide smile illuminating the chaos of freckles dancing across her cheeks. Kai's heart felt as if it stopped, and he knew he was doomed. His damn heart was falling fast, whether his mind threw out the warning bells or not.

"You look awfully deep in thought, music man," she joked. "Do I even want to know?"

Kai turned away, grabbed his car keys, and headed toward the front door. He would still spend the rest of the night with Bexley, but he seriously needed some space to get a grip on his foolish heart. "I'll meet you in the driveway. We'll take my Jeep," he said before rushing out into the cool night air. He needed some breathing room, fast.

Ten minutes later, Bexley strolled out, a cushioned cooler in one hand, her phone and some earphones in the other. "Ready for the next phase of our adventure?"

Kai couldn't help but smile. She was genuinely so happy and carefree that it was hard to stay closed off around her. He sighed, hopped into his Jeep, and cranked the gear into place as it rumbled to life. "Get in, firecracker," he said. "I told you already, I'm yours for the night. Let's go have some fun."

They wound their way along the coast and up into one of the swankiest neighborhoods of Laguna. There, high up on the cliffs, where the multimillion dollar homes kept vigilant watch over the beaches below, Bexley directed Kai into a long driveway that snaked its way toward the edge of the cliff next to an ultra contemporary white boxy home. Kai whistled, turning off the engine of his loud Jeep, which suddenly seemed so out of place.

"Whose house are we at?" Kai asked, looking around. "And are they gonna be pissed that we're showing up at almost two o'clock in the morning?" His eyes shot up to the floor-to-ceiling windows that seemed to frame the whole side of this house. He could only imagine the view from inside; he knew it would offer a spectacular panorama of the surf below.

"'Two of my favorite clients live here. Well, when they're in the states. When they're not, which is about half the year, I get to house-sit and take care of their cats, Fred and Ginger."

They walked toward the enormous arched white front doors, modern lanterns flanking each side and brightening the house as if it were daylight. There was white everywhere Kai looked. "Fred and Ginger? You have got to be kidding me," he snorted.

"Stop. They're gorgeous Bengals. Wait till you see them. I have to feed them and then leave my key. Someone else is taking over tomorrow. I've been watching them off and on for almost the entire year I've been here. I'm gonna miss them," she said quietly.

It dawned on Kai that these cats were probably the most permanent things in her life, even though they weren't even hers.

When they walked inside, Kai was speechless. The white surfaces of the gleaming tiled floors and marbled countertops overtook his view. Everything was white, or a soft version of it. The stairs, the contemporary low-back sofas facing gigantic windows, the walls, the fluffy pillows, and throw blankets. Kai was afraid to walk into such a sterile house.

Bex kicked off her sneakers and padded in barefoot, whistling softly for the cats as if she lived there. Kai chuckled when he stared down at her worn-in black Chucks, even as he kicked off his matching, larger pair.

He stepped down onto the cold marble floor. Despite the luxe decor, Kai's eyes could not leave Bexley. She'd sat down on a large, fluffy white carpet and was petting what looked like two leopards: one white and gray, and one brown and black. She looked up at him, pure happiness lighting her jade-colored eyes. "Come meet Fred and Ginger," she said.

Kai shook his head and walked over to where Bex was stretched out on the floor in the center of the room, all warm and tan and glowing—a stark contrast to the gleaming white that surrounded her. He sat down next to her on the lush rug, their legs brushing, and watched as the two cats sniffed him out. Kai had to admit they were awfully cute. "Let me guess, the white one's Fred, the brown one's Ginger?"

Bexley smiled. "Yep. But," she said dramatically, " Fred is the girl, and Ginger's the boy." She laughed at the look on Kai's face.

"That's so wrong. Poor Ginger probably has a kitty complex," Kai said, laughing as he reached out and pet Fred.

After feeding the cats, Bexley led him outside onto the enormous cedar deck that took up two levels of the backyard. There was an endless pool overlooking the ocean below, and long, modern lounge chairs that looked more like double beds lined the poolside, just like at a resort.

"Come here, you have to see this view," Bexley said. They walked to the edge and looked down at the crashing surf below. Bexley took Kai's hand in her own and they stood there for a moment, silent. "It's one of my favorite places in Laguna," she said.

"I can see why." His eyes took in miles of the coast in both directions. He turned to face her. "Is this something you want someday?" he asked, curious.

"The house? No. It's too big and cold for my taste. I like Madison's cottage-style home better. I mean," she said, sweeping her arm out at the home and the crystal blue pool next to them, "I can't deny it's gorgeous. But it's not my lifestyle. It's too . . . " she paused to think for a moment.

"Permanent?" Kai said, joking.

She elbowed him. "No, smart ass. I was just thinking that even if I settle down somewhere someday, I don't want my house to feel like an anchor. I wouldn't want my life to be consumed by a home this large and all the responsibilities it brings. I want a small patch of land for a little wildflower garden. I want maybe a thousand square feet, and a nice little screened-in porch. That's about it."

"You know you won't be getting that in New York City, right?"

Bex nodded, quiet.

"Sorry, I didn't mean it like that," Kai said. "Just being practical."

"It's not that," Bexley said. She let go of his hand and sat down on a lounge chair, patting the one attached to hers for him to join her. They lay down and looked up at the stars above them. "Have you ever heard the myth about how stars are long dead before we ever see them twinkling in the sky?"

She looked over at Kai in the dark, scrunching her eyes at him. Then she laughed softly. "Of course you have. You're a teacher."

Kai reached out and took her hand. He had heard people say this before, but he also knew it was just that—a myth. "Bex, I'm a music teacher, not an astronomer. Tell me what made you think of that."

"I was just thinking about how quickly people seem to want to believe that of course nothing that magnificent and incomprehensible could exist in its own beauty while it's still alive and pulsing. It's almost like they can't appreciate its beauty in the moment. It's easier to believe they've already died out, and we're just seeing a reflection of what once was."

Bexley looked down and picked at the hem of her shorts, as if trying to piece her thoughts together. "I don't know where I'm going with this... It just reminded me of my father. How suddenly, after he died, everyone wanted his unfinished manuscript. It's almost as if they couldn't appreciate his vast complexity while he was still alive. But by the time they could, it was too late. They were only chasing shadows, reflections of a man who once was."

She took a deep breath as she looked out into the vast darkness before them, the only light coming from the stars and the few hillside homes with errant lights on. "I feel like that's all I do, Kai," she admitted. "I've always loved traveling, loved the nomadic lifestyle my parents gave us. But sometimes I wonder if chasing all these dreams, all these sights, is a waste of time. Or, if I'm so busy chasing shadows, will I look back one day and wish I'd been able to see what's right in front of me? I've never been good at that."

"Well, you're about to put roots down now with your sister, right? When it matters most and she needs help running her business, you're going to be with her, even if that's not what's in your heart. That's pretty noble and brave, if you ask me."

Bexley bit the inside of her cheek, clearly noodling something. Kai was quiet, giving her the space she needed to work through whatever it was she wanted to tell him.

"It's not really as noble as it sounds," Bexley said. "My sister asked me to start the business with her, but I couldn't; it has always been her dream."

"What kind of business did you say it was?" Kai asked.

"A model management company," Bexley said, sighing. "I'm so low maintenance, Kai. I could live out of a backpack and a pair of Chucks for the rest of my life. Can you just see me dealing with needy, demanding models all day? It's definitely not *my* dream job."

"Then why are you going? Surely she would understand that it's not a right fit for you. And you're giving up your established massage therapy business, right? Aren't you passionate about that?"

"Absolutely. Though, like I mentioned earlier, I wanted to expand it someday," she admitted. "But it doesn't matter what I want. And that's why it's not noble. Kai, the only reason I'm going to help Vaughn is because she's dying."

The silence hung in the air like thousand pound weights pressing on Kai's chest. He closed his eyes, sadness filling his heart. He was so angry at the universe in that moment for taking Bexley's parents before their time, and then taking the only family she had left. It wasn't fair.

He squeezed her hand. "Bex—"

"It's okay, Kai. There's nothing to say. But if she weren't dying, I wouldn't be racing to New York to be with her. I miss her terribly, for sure, but that's the selfish gypsy side of me coming out."

"Bexley, it's not so black and white as you're trying to make it sound. It's not selfish of you to want to be happy and to follow your dreams, even if that has you moving around a lot and chasing new adventures. Hell, I wish I were half as adventurous as you," he admitted. "But when your sister really needs you—the only family you have left—you're going to her. You're sticking. That's pretty unselfish if you ask me, wild cat."

He leaned over and tucked a stray hair behind her ear. The rest of her red hair was pulled into a messy ponytail, and Kai longed to reach out and kiss that exposed smooth skin of hers.

"Bex," he whispered, "you know, you have this story ingrained in your mind as if it's set in stone. I think you wear these gypsy tendencies like a badge because your father was that way, and because he labeled you the same when you were just a child. But it doesn't mean you can't change—can't build a stable, beautiful life somewhere, even if it's across the country in New York. You'll be okay," he said. "You seem awfully resilient and happy to me. I think when you get there, it'll be like one new big adventure and you'll tackle it like you seem to have done with all the other challenges you've been confronted with in life. You're not just flighty, Bex. You seem brave, and strong, and beautiful, and smart to me."

Bexley didn't say anything; she crawled over the lounges and sat on Kai's lap, facing him. He swallowed hard. Not the reaction he was expecting, and he wasn't sure how long he could behave with her bottom pressing down onto his lap. He placed his hands on her hips as she lowered her forehead to his.

"How'd you get so fucking perfect?" she asked.

He laughed. "I'm far from perfect. I just know the sun when I see it. You are no long-burned-out star in the sky, Bexley, that's for sure. You're the biggest, brightest fucking light in the galaxy. I'm just a simple little planet orbiting you, hoping to get a little taste of your warmth before the eclipse."

She leaned down, inches from his mouth. "Oh, I'll give you a taste of my warmth, music man." She brought her mouth to his, tugging gently as she licked his full bottom lip. "Kai," she breathed out between kisses, "I don't know what it is about you, but you seem to see right inside of me like no one else has been able to do since I was a little girl. It both terrifies me and turns me on like nobody's business. But I can't change overnight. We hardly know each other, and I can't help my circumstances. My sister needs me, and I'm getting on a plane in"—she looked down at her Fitbit—"twelve hours."

"There's a lot we could get to know about each other in twelve hours," Kai said, his voice turning raspy as she leaned down and kissed the crook of his neck. She moaned against his skin and it nearly unhinged him. "But I'm not going to be able to think with you nibbling on my neck and sitting in my lap. You're making this awfully hard on me, Bex."

"Who said I'm trying to make it easy?" she purred.

"What's your favorite color?" he asked.

"Burnt orange."

"Burnt? What's wrong with fresh orange? Or raw orange? Or evenly cooked orange?" he asked, laughing.

"Because burnt orange is richer, has more depth, more passion than just regular orange," she answered matter-of-factly.

"Hmm. You've thought a lot about this," he said. "My favorite color is black."

"Black's not a color. It's the absence of color."

"Nothing's simple with you, is it Bexley?" he growled. "Maybe I do just need to kiss that sweet mouth of yours so you'll stop being so technical."

"Did you just say 'technical' while I'm sucking on your earlobe? That's kind of hot. Say some other big words to me," she joked as she lifted his shirt and placed her mouth against his chest.

Kai's mouth went dry. All he could feel was Bex's lips on his skin. The warmth of her tongue sliding over his flesh mixed with the cool night air shot spears of desire right to his cock. With her grinding her bottom in his lap, and her lips clasping onto his nipple, he was thinking of something big all right, but it certainly wasn't words. But if he didn't, he would seriously flip her over and fuck her brains out, right there on someone else's longue chair.

"Precise," he said, her tongue dancing across his pebbled flesh.

"Quantum," he groaned, feeling her mouth close around his nipple as her hand shot between his legs, rubbing him through his shorts.

"Abstemious," he rasped out, her delicate hands brushing over the tight bulge straining between them. "Bex, we need to stop."

"Just a few more," she whispered, her mouth moving farther down his chest to the top of his tight abs.

Christ. "Circumlocution."

"God, you're so sexy when you say big words to me," Bexley

said, laughter in her tone; yet nothing but heat was in her eyes as she looked up at him from his taut stomach. She'd now shimmied her way down his body and was leaving a trail of kisses along his tummy.

"Evanescent," he said, trying to focus on words and not the slick feel of her tongue. "Thermodynamics. Sanguine. Nomenclature."

She slipped her tongue down to the top of his shorts and licked beneath the material, dangerously close to his manhood. He fisted her hair. "Loquacious. And we're done with this game, Bex." He urged her up, bringing his mouth to hers, taking her, his tongue pushing its way between the soft flesh of her lips. He wished to God he could feel her mouth wrapped around him in a different way right now, but he wanted more than that with Bexley, and there was no way he was fucking her on someone else's pool furniture.

"When I finally make love to you, Bexley, we're gonna be done with these games. Make no mistake. It will be me, you, and your wide-open heart—or it will be nothing at all. Now, if you'll excuse me, I need a moment," he said, getting up off the chair and heading back to the house. Before he got halfway around the pool, Kai dove in head first, the lukewarm water not curbing the edge of his lust nearly as much as he'd hoped it would.

Damn, that girl.

chapter Nine

"Want to go on a little road trip?" Bexley asked as they buckled into Kai's Jeep. The deep rumble of the engine vibrated Bexley's whole body and set it even further on edge. She certainly wasn't a prude, but one-night stands weren't really her thing either. But never before had she wanted someone so quickly after a first meeting. Perhaps it was knowing this was her one and only shot with a man like Kai, since this was her last night in Laguna. All she knew was she was getting her shot in tonight. Come hell or high water, she wanted to feel the surrender of giving herself over fully to Kai before the night was through.

"A road trip?" Kai laughed. "We don't have very much time left for a road trip. Unless . . ." he trailed off and wiggled his brows at her. Bexley could tell exactly what was going through Kai's mind.

"No, I'm not skipping my flight," she said, laughing along with him. "Though I'd be tempted to if you promised to deliver on what's behind those wiggling eyebrows of yours." She winked at him and hiked a leg up on his dash. She watched as Kai's eyes inched slowly from her tattered Chucks, over her calves, along her thighs, and to the hem of her jean shorts. *Damn!* Bexley was getting wet just from the intense look in his eyes as they met hers. She'd felt as if his hand had slowly made its way along her skin, traveling the same route his eyes had taken.

"I could be persuaded, Bexley," he said quietly.

"Oh, could you now?" she teased. "You don't seem the one-night stand type."

"Who said it would be a one-night stand?" he asked, his hand reaching over and kneading her upper thigh where her shorts met her skin.

"You are relentless," she moaned, her head leaning back against the seat. "Drive. Now. Before I'm tempted to fuck you right here in your Jeep in my client's driveway."

She watched as Kai swallowed, hard. His fingers dug into her flesh a little tighter, but he let go. He jammed the gear stick in reverse and punched the gas, sending them flying backward down the long driveway leading away from the house. Bexley squealed when he pulled into the street and popped the Jeep into gear again, circling and tearing away from the pristine homes that lined the mountaintop.

"Okay, where to, Bex?" Kai asked as they wound their way back to town.

"Well, there's a town about twenty minutes away that I'd love to take you to. It has one of my favorite parks there. Oh, and an all-night tattoo parlor," she said nonchalantly.

Kai looked over at her, his brow raised. "Is that right? You thinking about getting some ink tonight?"

"I might be," she said quietly. "I have a few pieces from really big events in my life, and this feels like one of them. I'm getting ready to go start over somewhere new. I just want one last tat to remind me of the West Coast. What I'm leaving behind."

"Exactly how many do you have?" Kai asked, a mischievous twinkle coming into his crisp blue eyes. Bexley could tell by the lust that hooded his gaze that he was having a hard time keeping his vision on the road and not wondering where on her body the tats were. "And can I see them all?"

"Well . . ." Bexley dragged out. "Do you have any?"

"I might," he said, giving nothing away.

"How about a little game of show and tell then?" Bexley suggested, a smirk causing her lips to lift as she thought about searching his body for any ink he might have.

"Show and tell, or look and find?" he teased. "You look like a cat that just caught a mouse. Should I be afraid?"

"You should be very afraid," Bexley said, her hand finding its way to his thigh. She lifted the hem of his shorts, her fingers lacing along his skin as they inched farther up his leg. "I know just where I want to look first."

"Spoiler alert . . . I'm not the kind of guy to tattoo my—"

She swatted his arm with her other hand. "I didn't mean *there*. Though," she said, shrugging her shoulders, "I suppose I should look, you know, just to be thorough."

"I can promise you there's no ink there," he said, laughing.

"You're no fun," Bexley said and pouted. "What am I gonna have to do to loosen you up tonight?"

"You mean, more than make out in the ocean and let me slide my fingers up inside of you? Because I guarantee you, Bex, that's not my normal Saturday night."

Heat scorched Bexley's cheeks and she was glad Kai couldn't see it in the dark. "You got me there," she admitted. "Hey, why don't you get one with me?"

"Get one what?"

"A tattoo, silly! We'll each get one. Something to remember the night by."

"Bex, I can guarantee I'm never gonna forget this night. I don't need a tattoo to remind me of the night I met the most beautiful woman alive."

Bexley swallowed as she looked at Kai. His profile was every bit as intoxicating as his face head on. His nose was manly, but not too large. His chin was angular, and she found herself wanting to touch the hard lines of his jaw. Hell, she wanted to touch every inch of Kai's chiseled body. She wanted to go on that look and find search for his tats in a bad, bad way.

They made it to Mission Viejo in less than twenty minutes. Pavion was one of Bexley's favorite parks, and she couldn't wait to go be silly and explore it with Kai. She wanted to see if there was a fun, playful side to him, as well. So far she'd seen his serious side, his thoughtful and kind side, and his intense, sexy side. Now she wanted to see the playful side of Kai, and later, his adventurous side. Because she was determined for him to get inked too.

Theirs was the only car in the parking lot and Bexley was sure the park was officially closed, but she grabbed Kai's hand and wound her way over to the playground area. She raced over to the swings first, and hopped on. "Give me a push, will you?" she called out over her shoulder.

Kai laughed. "I wasn't expecting a park to be on our itinerary tonight," he said, pulling her back and giving her a big push. He settled onto the swing next to hers and rocked slowly as she pumped her legs and went higher and higher on her own swing. She threw her head back and looked up at the sky as she swung.

She felt so free on a child's swing. This park was so similar to one she had memories of going to with her father when she was younger. Perhaps that was why it was her favorite in the area.

Her father had taken her by the hand and led her to the swings. She hopped on and pumped her legs as best as she could for just turning five. Her dad pointed out constellations to her as she swung higher and higher. "Someday, you'll touch one of those stars, Bexley. You have it in you, you know, to do anything you want. Be anyone you want."

"What if I want to be a writer, just like you, Daddy?" Bexley asked.

"Writing's a fine job, but you can be anything you choose," he said. He cleared his throat, sounding hoarse. "Just never forget that no matter where you go in life, you can always look up at these stars and find your way home. Home isn't one place, Bex. It's who you share your life with. And we will always be under the same sky, my little Bexie Bean."

Bexley wiped the tears that threatened to spill over onto her cheeks. She missed her parents so much, and instead of getting easier with the passage of time, it felt as if it was getting worse. Maybe because she knew Vaughn was going to die soon, too. Bexley choked back a sob when she realized that after Vaughn was gone, there would be no one special in her life who shared the same sky, whom she could find her way home to.

She hopped off the swing without warning and ran up the planked bridge walkways that covered the kids' play area. She followed one to her favorite spot: the tree house. She could hear

Kai's steady footsteps behind her, but she didn't stop. When she got to the giant tree house, she fell to her knees and let her tears fall, her body shaking with the pent-up release.

When Kai's arms wrapped around her, she inhaled sharply at the familiar way he felt to her now. Comforting. She leaned back against him and closed her eyes, her chest heaving silently with the pain she'd been bottling up inside for so long.

"I'm sorry," she choked out. "Sorry for being such a hot mess tonight." Then she laughed, her giggle bordering on hysterical. "Not that you'd know how I was any other night—oh, fuck it. You know what I mean." Bexley lifted her shirt to her eyes and wiped the evidence of her pain away. *If only it were that easy.*

"Bex," Kai said quietly, running his hand over her hair from behind, "it's okay to cry. I can't imagine what you've gone through with losing both parents, and now knowing your sister is sick, too." He shifted her weight so she was curled up in his lap, her head resting on his chest. "Do you want to talk about it?"

"She has ALS," Bexley whispered. "I haven't told anyone yet, not even Madison and Josh. I don't know why, but maybe I felt like if no one knew, it couldn't possibly be real."

"What's ALS?" Kai asked, running his fingers along Bexley's arm and sending goose bumps across her flesh. It was meant to be a comforting gesture, but her body responded to even his slightest touch.

"Amyotrophic Lateral Sclerosis. Ever hear of Lou Gehrig?"

"The baseball player? Sure. Why?"

"Well, it's named after him. He died of it, and is one of the most well-known faces for the disease." She took a deep breath before going on. "It's a neurodegenerative disorder that affects a person's nerve cells in the brain and spinal cord, until eventually their muscles waste away. Vaughn started noticing a lack of feeling in her arms and it freaked her out, so she went to her doctor. After a lot of testing, and crossing off other diagnosises, they told her she has ALS."

Kai was quiet for a long time, just holding Bexley; the way their breathing was syncing up relaxed her even further, her tears now dry.

"You said it was fatal? There's no cure?"

"No," she whispered. "That's the hardest part. They are making such huge strides with research, but it affects everyone differently. Right now, there's no cure. She could live another six months, or another five years. But eventually, unless they find something new to test on her soon, she'll pass away." Bexley got quiet and traced circles on Kai's hairy arm with her finger. "The shittiest part is that your mind stays the same, but your body slowly gives out on you. That's why she needs me there. Eventually she'll lose all feeling in her arms and her legs. She'll need a wheelchair. Your voice—it goes too. Your throat can't swallow anymore, so she'll need a feeding tube, if she's lucky and lives that long." Bexley shook her head, unable to think of her vibrant, happy sister with no means to communicate, but trapped inside her failing body.

"And that's why you're going to New York, to take care of your dying sister . . ."

"That, and to help run her business for her until she passes."

"Have you thought about what you'll do with her business when she does?"

Bexley shook her head. She honestly had never thought that far out. She wasn't a planner like Vaughn was. The responsible one. This would be one of the biggest challenges of her life, and most days, Bexley was lucky enough to just be present and appreciate the day she was currently living.

"It's too far away. I know I have to think about it sooner or later, but I'll wait until Vaughn brings it up. In the meantime, I'll learn everything I can about her business so I can become her second hand." Bexley groaned. "Ugh. Literally." She couldn't help but let a small breath of nervous laughter escape her lips. It was all too much for Bexley to navigate right now, especially on top of her cross-country move.

"Okay, no more gloom and doom from me. Let's change the subject," Bexley said, sitting up and facing Kai. She crossed her legs, took a deep breath, and let it whoosh out. She shook her hands out at her sides and rotated her neck from side to side, trying to relax so she could lighten her mood.

"How many siblings do you have?" Bexley asked.

"None."

"Pets?"

"None, currently."

"Currently?" she asked.

"I want a dog, but I'm not home enough during the day. Don't think it would be fair."

"Fair enough. How come you wouldn't do a shot with me at the bar?" she asked. It hadn't escaped her how smoothly he'd dodged her question earlier.

"Damn. Noticed that, huh?" he said and gave her a sexy half-grin. "It's not really a big deal. I just don't drink anymore."

"Anymore? That means you used to."

"Congratulations, Sherlock," he teased.

Bexley playfully swatted him on the arm. "You know what I mean. Why don't you anymore? Is it a religious thing?"

"Nah, nothing like that. Just a personal thing," Kai said as he shook his head. Bexley could see his jaw clench as he consider his words. "I lost my mother to a drunk driver. Asshole was three times the legal limit and walked away from the accident. Let's just say that drinking's never held much appeal for me after that," he admitted, staring out across the playground. "It doesn't bother me when other people want to drink, though, but I'd never let a friend drive home intoxicated."

"I'm so sorry to hear that, Kai," Bexley said, squeezing his hand. "That just fucking sucks. You're right, though. Time doesn't really help much, does it?"

"Nope," Kai said, squeezing her hand back. "Sorry for breaking the no gloom and doom declaration you just made," he teased.

"That's okay. I just said no more gloom and doom stories from *me*. I never said you couldn't go there," she said as she winked at Kai. "Okay, so, back to my questions. What's your favorite music?"

Kai grinned, obviously relieved to move on to a new subject. "Man, that's a hard one. I was a music major, so I appreciate music all over the board."

"Name a few," Bexley said, loving the scowl of deep concentration that suddenly furrowed Kai's brow.

"Muddy Waters, Stevie Ray Vaughn, The Doors, Cobain, Indigo Girls, Freddy Mercury . . ." Kai took a breath and laughed. "Want me to go on?"

"Absolutely. I'm intrigued," Bexley mused. Her playlists ranged from Taylor Swift to Snoop Dogg, so she was in no position to judge. Plus, a person's playlist said a lot about them, and Kai had so many different sides to his personality that she found herself wanting to understand.

"Michael Jackson, Flogging Molly, Mayday Parade, the Cranberries—you remember them?"

Bexley pulled out her phone and plugged in her earphones. She handed one of the earbuds to Kai. They adjusted their bodies against the hard wall of the tree house, their legs dangling high above the ground, peeking out from small spaces in the faux wooden slats. As the haunting melody drifted through the earbuds, Kai reached his hand out and took Bexley's in his own.

"You know I'm such a fool for you / You got me wrapped around your finger . . ." Kai squeezed Bexley's hand as he hummed the line, the pad of his thumb rubbing back and forth over her hand.

"Here, may I?" he asked when the song was over. He scrolled through her playlist and selected another song. She laughed when he pulled up Reel Big Fish's "Take on Me" cover. *Nicely played, music man.* His eyes never left hers as they connected over the lyrics together. Yeah, the cover was intentionally cheesy; his selection, however, decimated her heart in ways she couldn't quite name.

They sat holding hands in the tree house for the next hour, taking turns picking songs for the other to hear. But a few simple lines from the first song they shared were the ones she couldn't shake; they were the ones that scared her the most and made her dread the end of their epic night in just a few short hours: "I just want to be with you / And I'm in so deep . . ."

chapter Ten

Kai was feeling quiet, melancholy, when Bexley played the last song for the night. She tried to turn it off, but Kai stopped her, enchanted by the haunting melody. It was a remake of "Let Her Go." Although the words didn't echo their—well hell, Kai couldn't even say "relationship." It was too new. Too impermanent. Kai's heart felt like the sands that had blown around their feet earlier as they raced across the beach. His heart was getting caught up in Bexley, and she was like a hurricane just tearing through. He knew then that he wouldn't escape this night without getting his heart destroyed.

Kai couldn't decide if it was really worth it.

Bexley took their earbuds out, gently, as if understanding the fragility of the moment after letting their hearts connect so deeply over music. It was like being seen truly bare for the first time. *"Love comes swift and it goes so fast."*

Kai didn't need to wait until he let Bexley go to know he would miss her. He already missed her, and she was kneeling in front of him, eye to eye, nose to nose, breathing slowly with him.

"Kai," she whispered. She put her hands on each side of his face and pulled back to look at him. "I'm scared. Okay? I'm scared about how I'm feeling with you tonight. I—"

Kai stopped her. It tore his heart to watch her grappling with what was happening when he couldn't explain it either. They'd only known each other for a few hours, he reminded himself. He needed to take a step back and chill the fuck out, not put so much pressure on the poor girl. Hell, she was leaving her life, her home, in just a few short hours.

"It's okay, Bex. Like you said earlier, you're leaving. We only have a few more hours together, so let's make them count." He leaned in and brushed her lips slowly with his, taking his time. He nipped at her lower lip, sucking it in and tugging it gently. "Do we still have time to play look and find before we go add a new tat to this beautiful skin of yours?" Kai moved his kisses from her mouth to her neck, where he ran his tongue along the soft flesh, loving the way she tasted, smelled. Like the summer waves, tropical sunshine, and fresh California oranges. He wanted to taste her fully, feel her dribbling down his chin like the citrus's juice. He wrapped his hands around her ponytail and tugged gently, exposing more of her neck to him, sucking hard at the delicate flesh of her clavicle.

"Where's the first one, Bex? Am I hot or cold?"

"Hot," she whispered. "So hot." Her hands pressed gently on his chest, gripping his shirt in her fists.

"Hmmm," he murmured, looking around her neck and throat. There, tucked right up under the base of her ponytail, he saw ink. He moved his lips over her neck and around the back of her throat, turning her so that her back was to him again. He lifted her ponytail to the side, and there at the base of her hairline was a blue lotus flower opening in front of a rising sun. How had he missed this earlier?

"A lotus flower, I like that. Very zen-like. Is that why you got it? Because of your massage therapy business?"

Goose bumps pebbled her skin as he traced the delicate lines of the flower. It looked more like a watercolor painting than a tattoo, very soft and dreamy.

"No, it actually means something else to me," she said, taking a deep breath. "Egyptians believed a lotus flower was similar to the sun, in that it sank down each night into the murky water only to emerge and bloom again the next day. For me, it represents that rebirth. It just felt right after my parents' accident. No matter how bad things were, I've always managed to rise again the next day, start anew somewhere else. Stronger. It also reminded me that no matter how afraid I was of being alone, there's something comforting about the predictability of the sunrise each day. The sun's going to come up, and I'll be okay, no matter what."

"It fits you," Kai said, letting his mouth come down and rest upon her tattoo. He slowly licked the skin around it, bringing his hands to her waist and pulling her against him. She leaned her head back against his shoulder and sighed. His hands slid up and down her arms, his fingers raking the sides of her breasts with each passing.

Kai kept his lips on her neck, her ear, her shoulder, until she turned into him, raising her lips to his. He bridged the distance to her soft mouth, their tongues meeting in a rush of heat. Kai could feel the vibration of the moan that escaped Bexley's mouth as they kissed. She arched her back and lifted her chest, inviting him to touch her, to feel more of her skin beneath his fingertips.

He cupped her breasts in both hands as their kisses deepened, kneading the soft mounds beneath the thin fabric of her T-shirt. When her nipples hardened and Kai realized she wasn't wearing a bra, he about lost it. He lifted his hips in response, pressing his hardness into her, loving the feel of her weight on his lap. She turned into him, twisting her body so she was facing him again. Her bottom pressed into his lap as she kissed him, her hands cupping his face.

It was Kai who groaned this time, his shorts tightening at every movement and gyration she made with her curvy little hips. He lifted the thin fabric of the front of her shirt, and the cool air against her flesh caused it to pebble even more. He brought his mouth down to one of her hard nipples, taking it into his mouth and tracing his tongue around the tight bud. Her hands were in his hair, hugging his head to her chest as his warm breath and teeth teased her skin, tugging and biting her nipples playfully.

"Number two," he whispered, as he traced his tongue over a Native American dream catcher to the right of her breast; he licked the beautiful blue feathers that trailed down her ribcage. "Wanderlust," he read aloud, kissing the word that danced in cursive from the center of the intricate circle. "What does this one represent?" he asked as he pinched her nipple in his fingers, rolling it gently.

She gasped, grinding her hips deeper into his lap. "It reminds me to chase my dreams, and how I'll always be protected. Kai—" she begged.

"Uh-uh-uh," he teased, flicking his tongue over her rock hard nipple. He ran it in a circle, and then pulled it in again, sucking it harder this time. He was rewarded when she ground very purposefully into him, almost willing him to enter her. *If only . . .*

"How many more?" he growled.

"Three," she whispered. "It's about to get interesting if you want to keep searching."

"I don't think I could stop now if I tried, baby," he said. He lifted her off his lap and set her onto the wooden slats of the floor, resting against the opposite wall. It was a tight space for two grown adults, but he shifted his body, his legs dangling out of the tree house's door. It gave him the perfect angle to lean forward and run a trail of kisses down the taut line of her stomach. "Am I hot or cold?"

Her body shivered as he circled her belly button with his tongue, plunging it in. "Hot," she croaked out.

"Front or back?" he asked between gentle sweeps of his tongue. Damn if he didn't wish this was something else he was licking.

"Back," she managed to rasp out.

Her hands weaved in and out of his thick, dark hair, alternating between playing with it and grasping it when his mouth was on her skin. It was a simple gesture, but it drove him absolutely nuts. He wanted to be between her legs, have them spread wide around his head, her hands tangled in his hair the same way as he plunged his tongue deep inside of her. If she tasted this amazing on the surface, he couldn't wait to taste all of her.

"Turn," he commanded.

She shifted in the small space for him, sitting on her knees. He slowly lifted the back of her shirt, but didn't see a tattoo at first. Then something caught his eye in the dark. At the top of her shorts the stem of a leaf peaked out. He ran his fingers along the rim of her shorts, tugging them gently. He wasn't about to take her clothes off in the park, in a kids' playset no less, but he was hoping to get a glimpse.

"Damn you," he growled.

She laughed. "I told you it would get interesting."

"Yeah, well, it's not getting interesting here. When I see that tattoo in full, it won't be in public, and I guarantee I'm going to want to spend some quality time worshipping it. I can't do that comfortably in here."

"Let's go then," she whispered. "Let's go get our tattoos, and then head back to my place. You can help me finish packing my carry-on bag. I've shipped everything else already, but I still have a few personal items I wanted with me this week. And I'd like nothing more than to spend my last few hours in Laguna making love to you."

The reality of her leaving was like a bucket of cold water thrown in his face. He trailed his hand along her waistline. She had a beautifully curvaceous bottom and her waist was small in comparison. He wrapped his hands around her stomach, dipping his fingers in the front of her shorts as he reached from behind. He leaned in and whispered to her.

"You won, firecracker," he breathed in her ear. "There is no way I'm letting you leave Laguna without making you mine, without knowing every single delicious inch of you. You wanted a one-night stand? You got one."

She shivered beneath his breath, and he wondered what was going on in her mind. All he knew was that it might end up just being a one-night stand for her, but this little gypsy girl had already rooted herself deeply under his skin. He would find a way to make this work. Her heart might be telling her to run and to keep things casual, but his was saying, "Damn, you're screwed, son."

chapter Eleven

It took everything in Bexley's willpower to pull away from Kai in the tree house and not let him take her then and there. The feel of his lips against her skin as he played look and find with her tattoos was almost too much to bear. They'd only known each other this one night, but everything in her was screaming for Bexley to get closer, instead of run away. It was so out of her comfort zone; but then he would kiss her again, pull her against his body, and all common sense was lost.

They made their way to Sunny's Ink & Drink tattoo parlor in silence, though Kai made a point to hold on to her hand the whole way there. Sunny's was Bexley's favorite tattoo shop on the West Coast because she could get inked by her good friend Sunny, and then toss back a shot of Fireball. There was only one simple rule at Sunny's, and it was etched onto a wooden surfboard above the front door: "No Drinking Before Inking."

The wind chimes on the door handle alerted her friend of their appearance before they could. Sunny came sliding around the corner into the foyer of her shop in nothing more than a pair of Wonder Woman socks, a teal bikini with a sheer cover, and a hug smile that lit her tan face. "Bexley!" she yelled in way of a greeting. She wrapped her arms fiercely around her friend for a full two minutes. Sunny was an affectionate soul, and Bexley was always down for one of her famous embraces.

Sunny pulled back to inspect Bexley and her guest, swinging her full head of dreads from side to side. They were pulled up into two long pigtails on each side, and were so blond they were nearly white by now. "Who do we have here?" Sunny asked. "This is the first time you've brought a boyfriend with you!"

Bexley sputtered and could hear Kai sniggering. "This is Kai. He's—well, I guess he is my boyfriend for the night at least. I leave for New York tomorrow, Sunny." Bexley looked at the clock on her cell phone. "I mean today. I leave this afternoon, actually. So," she said, trying to brush past Sunny's assumption, "thought I'd get one last ink to mark the end of my time on the West Coast. Can you squeeze us in?"

Sunny arched her overly tweezed brow at Bexley and waved

her arms around the empty parlor. "As you can see, we're swamped. But I'll kick all these bitches out to squeeze you in first."

Bexley laughed and hugged her friend again. "Man, I've missed you, Sunny!"

"So, are you both getting some ink, or just the lady with the balls?"

"Yes—"

"No," Kai answered at the same exact moment.

"So, just the lady with the balls then," Sunny said, her gaze pegging Kai to the spot.

"No, just the lady with the ink obsession. I hear she has five of them already."

"She surely does," Sunny said and smiled proudly. "Inked every one of them myself. Even the one—"

"Zip it!" Bexley yelled over Sunny, who gave her a puzzled look. Bexley bobbed her head toward Kai and said loudly in exaggerated Pig Latin, "Ixnay onyay ethay ocationlay."

Kai laughed out loud. "Oh, I'll find it, Bexley. Don't you worry about that."

Sunny nodded her head appraisingly. "Hmm . . . maybe he has bigger ones than I gave him credit for."

Kai looked back and forth between the two women, exasperated. "I'm right here! I can hear you."

"Well, Cinderella, if you're not getting inked, why don't you go wait at the bar?" Sunny suggested.

"I never said I wasn't getting inked," Kai said.

Bexley clapped her hands, jumping up and down. "Yay! I knew you wouldn't let me down." She flung her arms around his neck and gave him a great big hug.

Kai whispered softly into her ear, "Bex, I'll never let you down if you just give me a real shot."

She slid down his body slowly, their eyes meeting and holding. *Doomed. I'm fucking doomed.*

She turned to Sunny and said, "I want to it to be a surprise. Why don't you ink Kai first, and then me." Bexley looked at Kai, a seductive smile playing on the corner of her lips. "That work, music man?"

"Fine by me, firecracker," he said.

About ninety minutes later, they were perched on the antique metal swivel stools facing each other at the shop's bar, gauze covering their respective tattoos. Bexley looked down and noticed that Kai had gotten his on his left hand, on the side of his pointer finger. *What an odd spot*, Bexley mused. She had chosen to get hers on her left wrist.

Sunny grinned as she stood behind the bar. "Boyfriend for the night, my ass," she said, winking at Bexley. "Ready for a shot?"

"No thanks. We're done for the night," Bexley said, glancing at Kai from the corner of her eye. She turned to face him. "At the same time?"

He nodded, but didn't say anything.

"One, two," Bexley counted down. They both removed their gauze on three.

Bexley thought she would never be able to drag in a breath again. Her world tilted on its axis and her heart shattered when she looked down at Kai's small tattoo. It was a teeny firecracker in red, white, and blue on his pointer finger.

She looked up at Kai with tears dangerously close to spilling over, but then Bexley couldn't help but burst out laughing. "For this memorable adventure of ours on the Fourth?"

He closed the gap between them, his stool making a horrific screeching noise as he slid it across the concrete slab Sunny called a floor. "No," was all he said to Bexley, leaning in just inches from her lips.

She knew, but she dared not ask. She kept her eyes focused on his, afraid she would pass out if she didn't look away soon.

"It's all for you, firecracker," he said as he brought his mouth down onto hers, demanding more from her than he had yet that night. It was as if his kiss were a pen and he was signing his name on her heart, claiming it as his own.

"Kai," she whispered when they parted.

"It's okay. It'll make me happy when I see it. Every time I play the guitar, I'll think of you, and of our night together listening to music—"

"And other stuff," Bexley whispered.

"Yes, and other stuff. Like our impromptu swim at the cove. Our game of look and find. The way you snuggled on the floor with Ginger and Fred. How our tattered Chucks are almost identical," he said, snickering quietly. "Watching you laugh with your friends. And how you taste like summer and tangerines. And how, despite wanting to run from it, you have one of the biggest hearts I know."

Sunny cleared her throat from behind the bar. "Big ones," she whispered to Bexley, then walked back toward the supply room.

Bexley held out her wrist almost shyly now, showing Kai her ink. It was a bass clef and an upside down treble clef, joined together on her wrist to form a heart. "Music man," was all she whispered.

Kai swallowed hard, his intense gaze never leaving hers as he leaned in close, nearly grazing her mouth with his. "Girl, you are going to be my undoing," he whispered.

"Sunny!" she called out. "Put it on my card. Love you, girl, but we gotta run."

Sunny peered from around the corner of the supply room, her arms full of white towels. "Oh, I know you do, girl," she said to Bexley. "You call me the next time you're back in Laguna, okay? I'm straight up gonna miss you." She blew her friend a kiss.

"And you," she said, pointing to Kai, "make sure you never

lose those big cajones around that one. You'll need them with her. And, she deserves them."

"Yes, ma'am," Kai said, nodding his head toward Sunny. "It was nice to meet you," he hollered back to her, even as Bexley was dragging him from the shop.

As soon as they stepped out into the crisp predawn air, Bexley pushed Kai up against the brick wall of the tattoo parlor and pressed her body against his. Her hands found his hair again and she pulled his head down so their lips could meet. She kissed him hungrily, unable to get close enough to his skin. She ran her hands down the front of his shirt, feeling the hard outlines of the muscles beneath. She was growing damp just thinking of removing that T-shirt and having the weight of him pressed against her.

"Kai, come back to my place. Let's just spend the rest of our time together there. I want to feel you against me. I want to know you, Kai. All of you, before I leave."

Kai groaned, his mouth crashing down on hers, even as his hands found their way to cup her ass, pulling her firmly against the hard plains of his body. "Like I said, firecracker. You already won this battle. Take me home."

It took all of Kai's willpower not to drive a hundred miles an hour along the quiet highway back toLaguna. He hadn't had anything to drink, but it was a holiday weekend, so he drove with extra caution. It did not help to have Bexley's delicate little fingers running up and down the bare skin of his thighs. She had her head back against the headrest and her eyes were closed. She was humming along to whatever was playing on the radio, but Kai was so distracted with the thought of having his hands all over Bexley that he couldn't remember what was even on.

He squealed to a stop in front of the guest cottage and looked down at his watch. It was just after six a.m. He wasn't sure exactly what time she needed to leave, but he knew he didn't have as much time with Bexley as he wanted. He thought maybe she had fallen asleep on the car ride home, but a charming little smile lifted the corner of that wide mouth of hers. "Ready, music man?" she teased. She opened her eyes fully and climbed out the window of the Jeep, not even bothering with the door. Kai loved the way her shorts rode up, giving him a small glimpse of the curve he would find where leg met muscled buttock. He wanted to dig his fingers in her cheeks and pull her as close as he could against his body. He wanted all of her. Every inch.

If he was getting only one night with Bexley, it was one neither of them would ever forget.

chapter Twelve

Kai held Bexley's hand and followed her across the lawn to the small guest cottage. There were no lights on at the main house yet, so they snuck in quietly, giggling like teenagers afraid of getting busted. As soon as the door closed, Bexley kicked off her Chucks, grabbed Kai's hand, and led him into the kitchen.

"Come here," he said huskily before she could even turn the lights on. He grabbed her by the wrist and pulled her toward him. Their bodies collided together in a frenzy of fireworks that had all led up to this. He cupped the back of her head with his hand and met her clouded gaze. Lust swam behind those eyes every bit as deep and raging as his own.

"We are going to take our time tonight," he said, nipping at her earlobe. "I want you to remember every stroke of my hand, every lash of my tongue. Because you are not someone I'll soon forget, Bexley. And I want to torture you in every way possible before you leave today, so there's no way you can forget me either."

His mouth was on hers, his tongue dominating as his hands found their way into her hair. He yanked the ponytail holder from her hair, freeing it around her shoulders. "Yes," he murmured against her mouth. He turned Bexley around and bent her over at the waist against the small kitchen island where they stood. He wrapped his hand around her long, thick hair and pulled her up with it gently. His mouth found her neck and his tongue licked its way across her tender skin. He could not get enough of the way Bexley tasted.

"Jesus, Bex," he whispered in her ear from behind. "You taste like fucking oranges. I've never wanted an orange so badly in my life as I do right now. I want to taste all of you. God, I wish I could just bend you over and take you right here on the kitchen island," he growled. "Spread those legs of yours over my shoulders and devour you."

"Yes," she breathed out.

It stopped him cold. That wasn't what he was expecting. He wanted to take her back to her bedroom, take his time with her, go slow. Damn, she just would not let him have his way tonight.

He laughed. *Firecracker.*

He flipped her around so she was facing him and then lifted her in one swift movement so that she was sitting on the cold granite countertop. His eyes were trained on hers, and he loved the way her chest rose and fell . . . in anticipation? Excitement? He lifted her arms and pulled her small T-shirt over her head, her breasts bare and enticing right at his eye level.

He put both hands on each side of her legs on the granite and leaned in, pulling a nipple into his mouth without touching her. He heard her gasp, air rushing in between her parted lips. Her hands went to his head and she played with his hair just as she had earlier. He slid his tongue around the tight bud of her nipple, biting it, tugging it. She inched closer to him on the countertop, pulling his head to her body. He slid his tongue slowly down, toward the top of her shorts. She lifted her hips slightly as he edged them down, letting them fall to the floor. Damn if she wasn't wearing any panties either.

He knew she would be as wet as he was hard. But he wanted to take his time with her, maybe because of how much she was rushing things.

He brought his mouth very close to her ear but didn't touch it, so just his breath fell against her bare skin. "How does the cold granite feel against your warm bottom, wildcat?"

His mouth took in her earlobe, licking along the smooth folds of her skin and plunging inside. He let his tongue trail over her neck, down her clavicle. Her chest rose, begging to be cupped by his hands. He lifted both breasts, kneading them gently. They were the perfect size, her nipples so pink and perfectly round. They were so damn hard right now, too. He squeezed them, pulling them away from her body, knowing it would send shockwaves of pleasure between her legs. Her hips lifted in response, and he knew Bexley was just as turned on as he was.

"Kai, I want you to take me. Right now, here on the counter. I can't take this anymore," she whispered.

He leaned her all the way back against the granite. She arched her back as the cool stone met the warm flesh of her back. "Kai," she begged.

"Not yet. If I'm only getting you this one night, I'm tasting every single inch of you. And I'm not taking you on a fucking countertop. Not the first time, anyway. But I'll start here," he said, using his hands to spread her legs apart. He dragged his fingers up the crevice of skin where her legs met. "Is this a good place to start?" he teased, his fingers running along the outer edge of her lips.

He took a single finger and ran it up and down the opening. *So wet.* He smiled smugly to himself. He dragged the one finger up and down again, teasing her. His other hand was flat against her belly, caressing her soft skin. "What do you want, Bexley? Is this enough?"

"No," she gasped, lifting her hips to meet his hand.

"You want more? How about this?" he said, dipping his finger inside her wet opening. "And this?" he added one more finger on his next plunge in.

She bucked her hips and met his hand stroke for stroke as he brought her up, up, up. He pulled his fingers out and immediately brought his mouth to her warm folds. He breathed in her musky scent and dove in, running his tongue up and down the opening of her lips. He pushed her legs wider, and sure enough, she put them over his shoulders and it nearly drove him insane. He fucked that pretty little opening of hers with his tongue, harder and deeper until she called out his name, her hands clutching his hair as she orgasmed. She shuddered against his mouth as he licked her again and again until she was finished riding the wave of pleasure she'd experienced.

"Oh. My. God," was all she said, her hand flung over her eyes as she lay there, panting from the exertion and intensity of the climax. She giggled. "Holy shit, Kai."

He laughed with her, offering a hand and pulling her up to a seated position. "We're not done yet, wildcat. Come here," he said as he scooted her hips off the counter and to his waist. He walked with her across the small space and to the only other room in the small cottage, her bedroom. He set her down onto the bed and she rose to her knees, wrapping her arms around his neck as he stood there.

Her mouth found his just as heatedly, her hands fumbling to get his shorts down over his muscular hips. Her mouth dropped to his chest, sucking in one of his nipples. He'd never been one to be turned on by having his nipples licked, but maybe it was because every other girl had done it wrong. Because when Bexley did it, it made him twice as large in two seconds flat. All he wanted to do was to bury himself inside of her over and over again for the next six hours or so.

"My turn," she said, trailing her hands down his flat abs and toward his happy trail. His stomach veed there, and she took her hands and outlined the hard muscles that led down his hips and to his cock, which was hard and ready for her. She unbuttoned his shorts and finally slid them over his hips, letting them drop to the floor. Her eyes widened as she took him in, obviously pleased with what she saw.

He lifted his hand and touched himself, stroking the length of his cock. "You like what you see, Bexley? I want to feel myself buried inside of you before the night is over," Kai said. He'd never spoken to a woman as he was talking to Bexley right now, but she seemed to make him forget all of his inhibitions and good manners. He just wanted to take her, all of her, so badly. He reached for her hips, ready to push her back onto the bed and consume her.

"Uh-uh-uh," she tsked. "You wanted to go slow, remember, lover boy? Well, it's my turn now." She leaned down and wrapped her warm lips around his thick shaft. *Oh, dear God, she is going to unhinge me.* Kai dug his hands in Bexley's wild auburn hair that spread out around her head as she dipped and lowered, taking him in again and again, inch by agonizing inch. *At least when I die, I'll die with a smile on my face.*

Bexley wanted to make him come for her, but he wasn't having it. He tasted so good inside her mouth. She wrapped both hands around his girth and twisted her hands on his slippery cock as she took him into her mouth over and over again. Finally, he couldn't take it anymore.

"Bexley," he growled, "sit up. I want to know where those last tattoos are."

She looked up at him, her eyes full of feigned innocence. "You really want to see them now?" she teased, batting her lashes at him.

"Yes," he snarled at her. "Before I come in your mouth. Show me number three. I want to see the one on your back."

She let go of him and turned slowly on the bed, cupping her chest as she did, and booty-tootching her butt out seductively at him. She knew what he would find just above her bare bottom. Her "tramp stamp," as Vaughn called it. Bexley didn't care. She loved the delicate golden leaves and scrawling modern penmanship.

"Nothing gold can stay," he read, his finger trailing along the curve of her back where her waist arched in before giving way to her plump bottom. "What does that mean?"

She looked over her shoulder at him, their eyes meeting. "Nature's first green is gold. It's hardest hue to hold. Her early leaf's a flower, but only so an hour. Then leaf subsides to leaf, so Eden sank to grief. Then dawn goes down today—"

"Nothing gold can stay," he finished. "Frost. I thought I recognized that. Where's number four?" he asked after running his tongue over the series of falling leaves.

"Didn't you see it earlier?" she teased.

"Earlier, when?" he asked, then his eyes lit up. "Damn. How did I miss it?" He turned Bexley around and had her lie back against the soft mattress. She suddenly felt shy now that they weren't in the heat of the moment. It was one thing to spread your legs for a man when his mouth was on you, but another thing completely when he was looking at you so openly, so raw. She felt exposed, and it wasn't a feeling Bexley was either familiar with or comfortable doing.

He traced his fingers along her hip bone and down her leg toward her inner thigh, where a branch of cherry blossoms would forever bloom. There were two tiny butterflies dancing among the small pale pink blossoms, one blue, one yellow.

"This is beautiful, Bexley." His fingers touched one tiny, delicate petal at a time.

Bexley's skin pebbled, her insides tightening from his touch. God, she was insatiable when it came to Kai. "The Japanese believe the cherry blossom represents the beauty, but also the fragile brevity of life. Which is why the two butterflies are there. The blue one honors my father, and the yellow one honors my mother. Their lives were definitely examples of how fragile life can be."

He leaned down and kissed her tattoo, running his warm tongue the entire length of the branch. She felt as if the butterflies had flown into her belly and were giving chase. Her toes curled as he licked the sensitive dip of her hip bone. "Don't forget beautiful, Bexley. Life can be beautiful, too."

She murmured, and her fingers found his head again. They seemed to like it there, and they were getting familiar with the textured waves of his dark hair.

"Last one, firecracker. Give it up. Where is it?" he asked, his eyes grazing the length of her body until he met her eyes. "We have the neck, the chest, the back, the thigh . . . hmm." He sat up and lifted one of her legs into the air, his hands running slowly up her thigh, over her calf, and toward her foot. He twisted her foot this way and that and finally said, "Bingo!"

He squinted his eyes and moved closer to her big toe. Two vibrant blue fish were on the top, coming together in a kiss.

"What the—" Kai couldn't help but laugh. "What in God's name are these?"

"They're French angelfish," she said in way of explanation.

"Oh, they are, are they?" he teased. He lifted her foot to his mouth, kissing her toe delicately. "And they just happen to be kissing."

He took her toe into his mouth, sucking it all the way in. Spears of heat shot right up between her legs causing her to moan.

"Why, firecracker?" he said, popping her toe back in and sucking it harder as he massaged her calf.

Bexley thought she would come again right on the spot. She looked up her leg at him as he suckled on her toe, teasing her foot with his mouth. "They're angelfish. They mate for life. I like how they travel the sea together, but always only with one partner. It kind of gives me hope," she whispered.

Kai slowly released her leg to the mattress and looked at her. He shook his head as if she were a puzzle he couldn't quite figure out. He lowered his body over hers and cradled her head in his hands, bringing his mouth down to perfectly fit hers. He pressed his body against hers, and it was exactly the weight of him that Bexley was craving earlier.

He pressed the tip of his shaft against her wet opening and said, "Those angelfish, they're lucky bastards."

Bexley moaned as he slid inside of her, inch by inch, until he was tightly and deeply nestled. He moved slowly then, his eyes fixed on Bexley's as he found a steady rhythm that caused her to see exploding stars behind her eyelids. The last thing she heard before her earth-shattering orgasm was Kai's soft voice growling out to her, "I'll be your hope, Bexley. I want to be your hope."

chapter Thirteen

Bexley couldn't remember the last time she'd truly opened herself up and allowed herself the freedom and trust of an honest-to-God, toe-curling orgasm. Let alone three. In one night.

She smiled and stretched slowly, her frame brushing up against the cold sheets. Wait, wha—she looked around the bedroom and was disappointed to be alone. The room suddenly felt too quiet. Too empty.

She heard a rustling from the other room, so she got up and threw on her T-shirt before padding over the cool bamboo flooring to the main living area. There. There was Kai, leaning over the breakfast bar, looking out the back window of the cottage at all the lush greenery surrounding her small living quarters. Well, her old living quarters. In just a few hours, they wouldn't be hers to use anymore.

"Good morning, gorgeous," she said, walking up behind Kai and wrapping her arms around his waist.

"You mean, good afternoon?" he asked, turning into her arms and wrapping his around her, almost protectively. He leaned down and kissed her on the forehead. "You are so cute when you sleep."

"What? You watched me sleep? That's a little—"

"Romantic?" Kai asked, grinning. He reached for the coffee he had on the counter and took a sip from the oversized *Laguna Nights* TV show mug that was Bexley's favorite to use. It had a picture of Madison and Josh kissing on one side inside a cheesy blue heart, and #LagunaNights scrawled on the flip side.

"No, I was going to say creepy," she teased, poking him in the tummy. "But somehow you make it seem kind of sweet and, yes, romantic," she grudgingly admitted.

"Bex . . . I only get three more hours with you. I wanted to soak in every last detail. That's all. Don't read too much into it."

Oh. Okay then.

Bexley leaned in against Kai and inhaled deeply, wanting to memorize the way she felt in his arms, the way he smelled of trees and earth and sandalwood. "Hang on a minute. Don't move." She ran to get her phone and came back to find Kai pulling out croissants and muffins and bowls of fresh fruit from a grocery sack.

"Where did you get all that?" she asked.

"Madison dropped it off about thirty minutes ago. Told me to tell you that Francie was awake all night throwing up and woke up pulling at her ears. She has to take her in to the pediatrician's office, so it looks like you're getting a ride to the airport from me," he said, grinning. "I think she felt bad and this is her peace offering."

"Slick," she said. "Wait, before we eat . . . I just want a quick selfie. The lighting is so good in here and I want at least one picture of us," she admitted.

"Won't that just be torture?" Kai asked. "I know it will be for me."

"Maybe. But I think it'll be worse to know I'll never see your face again," she said quietly.

"Bex, you're moving across the country, not across the world. They do have things like, oh I don't know, airplanes, and Skype. Text messaging, SnapChat. You can definitely see my face again if you want to. This doesn't have to be goodbye, babe." He pulled her toward him, taking a deep lungful of air as he nestled his face in her morning bed head. "Mmm . . . morning oranges. I could eat you right up."

Bexley turned and leaned against his chest, pulling her phone above both of their heads for the perfect selfie. She took it right as Kai was leaning in to inhale the scent of her skin at the crook of her neck. She hated that she couldn't see his eyes directly, but she loved the dark slope of his hair, and the naughty little grin that peeked out just for her as if only they had a shared secret.

He lowered his lips to her shoulder and kissed her skin, then ran his tongue over it as his hands went to her waist. "What time is it?" he asked.

She looked at her cell phone and groaned. "Twelve thirty," she answered. "I have to leave in about two hours and still haven't thrown my last things into my carry-on."

"Shh," Kai whispered in her ear. "You have plenty of time. We have plenty of time," he reminded her, his hands slowly dragging down her sides and over her hips, pulling her back against him so their bodies were pressed together. "Bex, I'm going to miss you."

She turned into him, desperately searching his mouth, wanting to taste him one last time. *It's not fair, damn it!* she screamed inside as she started tearing away layers of his clothes. She just wanted one more day with Kai. Just one more day.

Kai sensed her urgency and met each stroke of her tongue with the same heat and longing. "Can I take you on the kitchen counter now, wildcat?" he asked. "It's all I could think about this morning. You, that fair skin of yours, and all that cool granite."

Bexley moaned against his mouth. "I'll take that as a yes," he said.

Kai lifted her wrinkled T-shirt over her body and pushed her back up against the countertop near the sink. Lowing his head he found her nipple, sucking it in hard, his hands running up and down her muscular back as he did. He bit the tip gently, tugging it, eager to be inside of her. He hated to rush it, but they didn't have a lot of time left.

Kai turned her around and moved her hair off her shoulder, kissing the base of her neck. He lowered her torso so her chest was lying flat against the slick surface of the countertop, then ran his tongue down the length of her back and to her backside. Cupping both of her cheeks in his hands, he brought his lips to her soft, giving flesh. He kissed one cheek, then the other, drawing her skin into his mouth and sucking hard. She pushed herself back against him, eager to be closer as he kneaded both of her ass cheeks in his hands.

He spread her legs with his hands, finding her wet opening with his fingers. Skillfully, he circled his thumb over her clit, rubbing it until he got the low moan he craved from Bexley. Sliding his hand back and forth against her, he could feel how wet she was already. Dipping two fingers inside, he found a slow and steady rhythm. She bucked her hips back to meet his hand, crying out his name this time. Kai removed his shorts and stroked himself, already hard from watching her take pleasure.

He just wanted one more taste of that succulent sweet orange before she left. He dropped to his knees and inhaled her scent. She smelled like cloves and sex. Kai buried his face inside her, while sending shockwaves through her body with his fingers.

"Kai, now, please," she cried. "I need to feel you inside of me."

He stood, grabbing her hips. "God, I've been waiting all morning for this, Bex," he said as he slid deep inside of her.

"Yes!" She pushed back against him, pulling him in even more.

She was tight, so damn tight around him. He held onto her hips and found a steady rhythm, matching the intensity of her desire. She was his sweet nirvana, sending him over the edge only when her insides clenched around him and she cried out his name as she came. He shuddered, falling against her back and kissing it, tasting her sweet perspiration from their exertion.

"It's a good thing you're moving, Bexley," Kai said.

She laughed. "Oh yeah, why's that?" She glanced over her shoulder coyly at him.

"Because all I'd want to do is fuck you every single day. I'd never get any work done. I'd lose my job. End up homeless," he said.

"Is that so?" she teased. "You have such smooth pillow talk, music man. Well, I guess it is better that I'm leaving then. I wouldn't want to be your downfall or anything."

Suddenly it no longer seemed funny to Kai. He pulled out of Bexley and drew her into his arms. "Why do I get the feeling you already are, wildcat."

Bexley didn't have time to contemplate how much fun she'd had with Kai, or how much she would really miss him now that she knew him—and knew every intimate inch of his body. He was a happy accident, one that she hadn't been expecting the night before. And when they'd first met, this—going to the airport today and leaving Laguna for good—well, it still seemed like a breeze. Just another step on her journey to somewhere else.

Now?

Bexley felt a little sick to her stomach as she packed the last of her clothes and toiletries into her small suitcase. They stood silently in the little cottage before they left for the airport.

"You know, I've spent my whole life moving around. It's never bothered me before. I've always looked forward to the next adventure, the next challenge. And before today, I thought I could do this. I thought I could walk away and not look back. Now," she said, bringing her eyes to Kai's, "I'm going to miss Laguna. I'm going to miss my walks with Madison and Annie. I'm going to miss taking Francie to the park and sneaking ice creams cones together." She laughed. "I'm going to miss my massage therapy clients. Everyone who came into the hotel was so generous and appreciative. And I'm going to miss those damn cats, too."

Bexley looked around the small space. She hadn't lived there long; she never did. But this tiny cottage had grown on her. There was good energy in the space, and she prayed her next home would be just as inviting.

"Kai," she began. Hell, Bexley didn't really know what to say to him. How did she thank someone for sweeping into her life unexpectedly and then turning it and her heart upside down—all in one night?

"You . . . were unexpected," she said, chuckling quietly. "To say the least."

She reached out and held his hand in her own. "Thank you for last night. For giving me a night I'll never forget." She lifted her wrist and smiled down at her tattoo. "For listening."

"Bexley—"

"I still can't promise anything, Kai. I told you that when I met you. I don't know what the next six months of my life are going to look like caring for Vaughn, and learning her business. Fuck," she said, raking a hand through her long auburn hair, "I know nothing, and I mean nothing, about the modeling business. I am starting from the ground up. And Vaughn . . . you don't know Vaughn. But she does nothing halfway. If I know her, she's already created an empire."

"Bexley, take a deep breath. You'll do great. Look at me," Kai said, lifting her chin so her gaze rose and their eyes met. "You are a fighter. You think you're just some flighty soul, but you're not.

You stick in ways you don't even know. You make friends, you change lives. You matter. Don't go to New York and just get lost in your sister's life. Promise me that you'll live your own. That you'll find something that makes your soul happy, and lets it shine. New York is not going to know what to do with you, Bexley Rue," he said, half-joking.

He lowered his lips to hers and kissed her softly. "I'm not asking you to promise me anything. We had one night, Bex. But it was one of the best nights of my life," he admitted.

"Hey," Bexley said, suddenly remembering, "we never played look and find on you!"

"That's because you have so many it took me all night," he joked.

"Stop!" She grew serious. "Can you just tell me where they are? I think I was so orgasm-induced last night I may have glazed right over them."

Kai laughed, lifting her chin so their mouths could meet again. He kissed her slowly, bringing his hands to the sides of her face. When he pulled back, he said, "You're hot."

She chuckled. "Gee, thanks. So are you."

"No, I mean, my tattoo. You're hot."

She looked around and saw the firecracker on his hand and grinned. "One," she said, kissing it.

"And only," he replied.

Bexley stared at Kai for a minute, unable to process that he got his first tattoo with her, for her.

"There will never be another firecracker like you, Bex. Just promise me one thing. Promise me you won't close the door to this—to us—forever. Let me say hi from time to time. See how you're doing in the Big Apple. And I'm here for you if you need anything, okay? I know you're not used to sticking, and I know the timing isn't right, but, Bexley Rue—I'm addicted to you, baby. And you're gonna be a hard, hard habit to break."

"Did you . . . did you really just say goodbye to me with cheesy song lyrics from the eighties?" she asked and laughed.

He grinned. "I sure did. You're worth it."

She snuggled against his chest. "Thank you, Kai."

"For what?" he asked, running his hand through her long, soft hair one more time. After her shower it smelled like oranges and vanilla, and he wished to God they had just thirty more minutes together.

"For being you. For understanding. For not pushing. For being a big old cheese ball."

He laughed. "You're killing my rep here, Bex. Come on, let's get you to the airport before you really do me in with your romance and I start bawling."

She punched his arm, pulling away. "You suck," she said, laughing.

He twirled her back to him and brought his mouth down hard on hers, crushing her lips beneath his one last time. "Yes, yes I do. And don't you ever forget just how good I am at it."

She grinned at him and said, "Trust me, that's not something I'll be forgetting anytime soon, music man." She picked up her purse and looked around one last time. "Bye, Laguna. You've been good to me," she said. Then she turned and did the thing she was best at: she walked away.

chapter Fourteen

Bexley couldn't find the invoice and it was pissing her off. She flipped the new bangs out of her eyes that she'd chopped off with most of the rest of her hair when she arrived to New York three months ago and had needed a change. Goodbye was the beach-loving, free-spirited Bexley. In her place was a slightly frazzled but take-charge kind of woman who was learning the ropes inside and out, and loving every minute of the new business she was running.

It had surprised Vaughn almost as much as it surprised Bexley. She missed Laguna, and her friends, but she loved the energy of the city, and the models she'd met were way more laid back and down to earth than she'd ever imagined they'd be. But between keeping up with her sister's doctor's appointments, learning her way around the subway system, and just figuring out where was good to eat, she had little energy left to miss her old life.

Laguna seemed like a lifetime ago. Bexley supposed that's what made it so easy for her gypsy soul to move on in the past; she was used to starting over with a vengeance.

She missed Kai more than she thought she would, especially those first few weeks as she settled into her new digs. A smile would spread across her face whenever she heard a familiar song they'd shared in the tree house together. But as the days passed, and Vaughn relied on her even more, she had less time to daydream about her one night spent with Kai. It was in the evenings though, when her world quieted and there was nowhere left to run, that his face came into her mind. The memories of his hands on her, his mouth, his very soul . . . well, let's just say she'd had many restless nights in New York. No vibrator in the world could replace the way she felt under Kai's skilled touch.

"Bex?" she heard from the doorway, nearly dropping the stack of papers she was leafing through. Her sister was there in her wheelchair, a file folder on her lap.

"Vaughn! I didn't know you were coming in today. Who brought you?" She walked over to her sister and bent down to hug her. Vaughn's speech was starting to slur, but Bexley could still understand everything she was saying . . . for now.

"My aide. Hey, can we talk?" she asked quietly.

"Sure, come on in," Bexley said, moving out of her sister's way. Vaughn pressed the button on the cord in her hand and the wheelchair moved forward, rolling in until it nearly hit the front of Bexley's desk. Their office wasn't in the best part of town yet, but Bexley was just grateful to have a window in her office that afforded her a street view of the vibrant city beyond their office walls.

"You look like crap," Vaughn said. "When was the last time you ate?"

"Gee thanks, sis. And how are you today?" Bexley asked, crossing her arms over her chest.

"I'm serious, Bex. What's going on?"

"I'm exhausted, okay? I'm running around trying to learn a new city. I'm walking everywhere. I am staying up too late trying to learn this business and the players. I'm taking care of the apartment so you don't have to do anything but rest. I'm just exhausted, okay?"

"No . . . it's not okay. It's more than that. You have bags under your eyes, Bexley. Like you haven't slept in weeks. Is this too much? You'd tell me, wouldn't you? If this isn't what you want to do? If you hate it here?" Her sister's voice caught, and Bexley felt like shit for even raising her voice an octave at her sister.

She plopped down into her desk chair and swiveled it, placing her feet on her messy desk. "I don't hate it here, Vaughn. I just . . ."

"Miss him?"

Bexley paused mid-swivel and looked out her office window to the bustling street traffic walking by. "Yeah. I miss Kai—more than I thought I would. He's so sweet though. I wake up most mornings to a text message or a funny SnapChat. He created a playlist for me of songs he wants me to listen to that mean something to him. He's just so . . ."

"Perfect?" Vaughn asked, smiling. "So what's holding you back?"

"Vaughn, it's just the timing, okay? We live on different coasts. And I have too much to juggle right now to let my heart wander again. I've spent enough of my life roaming and following my heart wherever the next breeze blew in from. I'm actually proud to be here right now, and for sticking. I want to be here, Vaughn. I've missed you. And right now, all of this is enough. I'm content, truly."

"But you still miss him," Vaughn whispered.

"I do. I don't know how it happened, but damn if he didn't slip into my heart somehow," Bexley said, looking down at her tattoo.

"Well, you never know what's going to come next. Don't count your love story out just yet, sis," Vaughn said, grinning. "By the way, were you looking for this when I came in?" she asked, nodding to her lap where the file folder rested.

"Is that the Prescott file?" Bex asked, eyeing her sister's lap with sudden interest. She leaned across the desk and snatched the folder from her sister—not that Vaughn could've stopped her.

"It is. His latest invoice is in there. He loved the mermaids idea and said he wants to move forward with it at his next bash. Do you have any girls who could pull that off?"

Bexley pumped her fist, excited that her first big idea was so easily accepted by one of their largest clients. If she knew one thing about Maximillian Prescott III, it was that he would want only the best. She chewed on the end of her pencil as she thought. "I have just the girls! We got two new models last week from another management company that folded. I snatched them right up and offered them full contracts."

"Wow, they must be something," Vaughn said, sounding a little forlorn.

"I'm sorry, did I do something wrong?" Bexley asked. "I thought you wanted me to start expanding our business whenever I saw a chance. Vaughn, these girls were too good to let go."

"No, I trust you. Who are they?" Vaughn asked, interest returning to her eyes.

"Their names are Layne and Gemma. Layne's all sexy-sweet girl next door, and Gemma is a Balinese beauty. Mr. Prescott will appreciate them both, I guarantee it."

"Fine, you handle it. And don't forget to send that invoice to his record label. We need the money coming in as quickly as it's going out."

"I'm on it," Bexley said. "Anything else? How are you

feeling today?"

"Well, that's actually what we need to talk about." Vaughn looked down at her hands, which had been folded on her lap for her. Bex knew she was having a harder and harder time moving her arms, and was worried that, soon, even getting around in the wheelchair was going to be an impossibility.

"Do me a favor?" Vaughn asked.

"Sure, anything," Bexley said, trying to make her sister smile. She didn't know how Vaughn did it every day. Got out of bed. Kept moving forward with life. Bexley was afraid that if their places were reversed, she would want to just curl up in bed and die. It was so hopeless, and Bexley didn't know how to deal with it most days. So she kept busy, let Vaughn's home health aide take the lead on most things, and kept putting one foot forward to learn something new with the business every day. She could not—would not—think about how long Vaughn had, or what she would lose next.

"First, can you move this hair out of my face?" Vaughn asked. "It's driving me nuts."

Bexley laughed, but walked around her desk and lifted the ash blond hair from her sister's face and tucked it behind her ear. Her aid had helped Vaughn with her makeup today, and she looked almost like her old self. "Now what?"

"Now, we sit and talk."

Uh-oh. Bexley did not like the sound of that. "Well, I have this invoice I need to submit, and I need to contact Layne and Gemma now," she said, looking around her office for even more to come up with. She did not like the sound of *we need to talk.* It gave Bexley the heebie-jeebies.

"You have to promise me you will go see a primary care physician, like, this week. Okay, Bexley? Seriously. You look like your iron's off or something. You're freaking me out. I can't have you scaring the clients."

Bexley shrugged. Vaughn had a point there. "Deal. If it will get you off my back."

"It will. When did you eat last?" she pressed.

Bexley shrugged again. "Yesterday? Lunch? I had a coffee this morning. Tried to eat a muffin but couldn't hold it down. You know how disgusting that subway smells. Think it was just the lack of sleep and the foul and mysterious odors down there," she joked. She stopped laughing when she saw the concern in her sister's eyes.

The fact that she was dying and still concerned for Bexley's health made her feel small. "Sorry. I don't mean to be flip about this. I will. I had my coffee, and it's almost noon. I'm starting to feel better and could use some fresh air. I'll go grab a sandwich. Maybe sit out in the sun," she said, suddenly energized at the thought.

"Good. Now, onto the harder stuff. We need to talk soon

about my end of life plan," Vaughn said, her gaze never leaving Bexley's. "I know you don't want to have this conversation, but we need to, and it's getting too close to ignore. It's time, Bex. I can feel myself losing more mobility every day. I have to have control over the details before I die; you know I do."

The room started to spin on Bexley. *No, no, no!* It was too soon for "the talk." She'd successfully avoided it every time Vaughn wanted to bring it up. But she saw the look in her sister's eyes. Saw the way her hands no longer moved on their own accord. Or her legs. They were getting weaker and weaker every day. She hadn't wanted to admit how much the aide was doing to help Vaughn move around now.

The last thing Bexley remembered was leaning over and throwing up the meager contents of her stomach into the trash bin. Then her world went dark.

chapter Fifteen

Kai was having a hard time concentrating at school lately. Every day, the first thing he thought of when he woke up was Bexley. That auburn hair, her adorable freckles, those green, green eyes. It didn't help when, the day after she left, he looked at his phone and found the picture he'd snapped of her the instant they met. She was so damn fiery and full of life. So much of her personality came out in that one closeup shot he'd taken of her. It seemed to suck the life right out of him and punch him in the gut every time he looked at it. Yet he couldn't stop.

What I'll never fully have, Kai thought and sighed.

He threw on some running sneakers and headed out into the bright Sonoma sunshine. Though it was autumn already, the temperatures were still in the eighties, and the sun was warm on his skin, as he ran through the town's square and into the adjacent neighborhoods boasting multimillion dollar craftsman-styled homes. They were off the main road, and the peaceful quiet afforded him some breathing room. Bexley's face came into his mind as he clipped out a steady pace. It wasn't too hard, considering he was listening to the playlist he'd created for her.

Yeah, they lived on opposite coasts, but Kai knew he had to find a way to see her again, and soon. He was going completely crazy after having had a taste of Bexley and not getting to hold her every day or talk whenever he wanted to hear her voice. They sent text messages almost daily, and exchanged funny SnapChats, but there was no mention of their situation or what the future held. He knew Bexley was up to her eyeballs trying to learn the ropes in a new city, running a booming business, and caring for her sister. It had to be emotionally draining, and he didn't want to be one more thing to burden her.

So he kept how deeply his feelings were growing to himself, and waited patiently until Bexley was ready to face the truth of what was developing between them.

His phone's ringtone alerted him to a new call, so he slowed to a stop as he checked the caller ID. He didn't recognize the number, but something told him to pick up the phone and answer it. He rarely got calls this early on a Saturday morning, and a hint of panic started brewing in his belly.

"Hello?"

"Hi, is this Kai?" he heard from the other end of the line. He didn't recognize the voice though.

"Yes, this is he. Whom am I speaking with?" he asked cautiously.

"Oh my God. I'm so glad I got through to you! It's Bexley's sister Vaughn and—"

"Whoa, whoa, whoa! Wait a minute. This is Vaughn? Where's Bexley? Is she okay?" Kai was having a hard time understanding her, as she was slurring her words.

She took a deep breath and seemed to be trying to annunciate better, though Kai hated to admit he was still having a hard time understanding her. "Yes, it's Vaughn. Bexley is at the hospital. I, I hate to ask you this, but I think she's going to need you by her side later today if she's released. Can you come?"

Kai put both hands on his knees and buckled over at the waist. Bexley was at the hospital? He took in a few deep lungfuls of air, trying to steady his panic and breathing.

"Kai? Did you understand me?" Vaughn asked. "Are you there?"

"Yes, sorry. You said Bexley is in the hospital, right? But she's getting out today you think?"

"Yes."

"Is she okay?"

"I believe so. They're running some tests to make sure. She's just exhausted and run down. She's been pushing herself too hard lately, not eating enough. She's anemic right now, and . . . well, I think she could use seeing you." Vaughn paused. "I haven't told her I was calling you though. I don't want her to get mad. But sometimes an older sister knows what's best. She's going to need you right now, Kai. And I don't know how much I can do to support her, you know . . . with my symptoms getting worse and all."

"Okay . . . so she's okay though," he said, more to reassure himself. "Yes, I'll get on a plane today. I'll text you when I get into LaGuardia. Can you send me your street address? She's still living with you, right?"

"Yes, thank goodness. My ALS is progressing much faster than we expected. I'll have Mary Jane, my aide, text you our address. Can't use my hands for much anymore," Vaughn said, trying to come off light, but Kai could hear the deep sadness in her tone. Hell, he couldn't blame her.

"I'm sorry to hear that, Vaughn. I'm looking forward to meeting you. Thank you for calling me. I want to be there for her if something is going on."

"I figured you would, Kai. That's why I called. You love her. She needs you here whether she knows it or not. She's a damn feisty and proud one, and sometimes she doesn't just let herself receive help. I wish I could do more for her."

Kai stood back up and looked around the quiet neighborhood.

He had to get home fast, pack, call the school, book a flight . . . a million to-do's were running through his mind. Then he stopped cold. Did Vaughn just say he loved Bexley? He ran his hand through his dark, wavy hair, warm from the morning sun. *Do I?*

"I'll be there, Vaughn," he said, neither confirming nor denying her choice of words.

It was a long run home, but he made it in record time, sprinting most of the way. Kai would be there for Bexley, whether she realized she needed him or not. Maybe this was a sign. Kai had been sitting in California on his ass for far too long. He missed the hell out of Bexley Rue, and nothing would stand in his way from getting to her now.

Kai made it to New York in record time, but because of the time zone difference, it was too late to go barging into Vaughn and Bexley's apartment. He had texted Vaughn during his layover and told her he would call in the morning to arrange a time to meet up with them. Vaughn's aide called him back to let him know that Bexley was doing better and was resting at home, per her doctor's orders. It gave Kai a little solace knowing she wasn't dismissing the incident entirely. Apparently, she had passed out in her office earlier that morning. The thought of Bexley being in such a vulnerable state scared the hell of him. He'd had a lot of time to think—and listen to their songs—on his flights from California to New York.

By the time he'd landed, he finally admitted to himself that he did, in fact, love Bexley, and damn if he hadn't since their first night together. She'd snuck in and consumed every little space in his heart, every inch of his lungs; every cell and every molecule inside his body seemed to function in tune to Bexley's presence in his life. His body breathed and pumped her as if she were the very air he needed to live. How he'd gone three months without physically seeing her or holding her, he had no clue. But Kai was determined to end this ruse now. He needed to find out where Bexley's heart was, and he needed to find away to permanently get on the East Coast, a.s.a.p.

He slept poorly in his hotel room. It wasn't in the most expensive part of town, as his budget wouldn't allow it. So he heard every car horn, every rumbling passing train, every note of soulful music that played into the wee hours of the morning. It was a little colder in New York than back home, so Kai opted to run on the treadmill when he awoke. He needed to burn off some of the energy that was building at the thought of seeing Bexley again. He downed a huge breakfast of bacon, eggs, French toast, fresh oranges, and a straight espresso. He was pacing his room when he finally got a call from Mary Jane.

"Hi, Kai. Vaughn asked me to sneak out and call you so that Bexley wouldn't hear. She is going to get her sister out into the fresh air this afternoon and do a picnic in the park. Could you meet us there?"

"Sure, which part?" Kai asked, knowing Central Park was huge, and he didn't want to risk missing them.

"Bexley loves the Conservatory Garden. You enter through the Vanderbilt Gate at 5th Avenue and 105th Street. Her favorite part is the South Garden, so just look for us there. Make a left when you come in and head toward the Burnett Fountain. Vaughn is in a wheelchair these days, so I think you'll be able to spot us fairly easily. And you have my number if you get lost."

"Thank you so much, Mary Jane. I'll meet you there in just a little bit."

Kai hung up the phone and jumped in the shower, his energy refreshed despite his restless night. He was going to see Bexley today, so his heart was truly happy for the first time in months. As he lathered up, he couldn't help but remember the way Bexley's hands felt on his skin, or the way she came for him when they showered in her little cottage together right before they left. It wasn't the physical closeness they'd shared that made Kai miss Bexley so damn much, but as he got closer to knowing he was going to see her in the flesh, it was suddenly all he could think about.

Today was going to rank up there as one of the best days of

his life . . . right after the first night he'd met Bexley, on her last night in Laguna. He grabbed his things and shoved them into his city backpack, eager to get to the park—and back home to where his heart belonged.

chapter Sixteen

Bexley awoke the next morning groggy and still reeling from her blackout the day before. Fuzzy pieces were coming back to her, though she was easily shutting out the reality of the situation, too afraid to face everything head on just yet, especially when her sister needed her most right now. *Fuck! Fuck! Fuckity fuck*, Bexley yelled in her head.

She got up and padded into the kitchen of Vaughn's small, but trendy, apartment. Bex had to admit, though not her usual style, the place was pretty darn cool. She was glad now that her other loft had fallen through; she hadn't been prepared for how quickly Vaughn's body would give out on her, or how much she would need Bexley's physical presence most days. Yes, they had Mary Jane to help, and she was a godsend. But there was something about having family around that made even the toughest challenges easier to face. Bexley was grateful for Vaughn's presence right now, too.

Vaughn and Mary Jane were sitting in the bright morning sun at the kitchen table, playing Uno. Well, Mary Jane was flipping all the cards for both of them, but Vaughn looked happy. Bexley walked over and gave her a sister a kiss on her forehead.

"So, who's winning?" she asked.

Mary Jane rolled her eyes. "Even in a wheelchair, unable to flip her own cards, this one is spanking me hands down. Sheesh," she said, grumbling good-naturedly.

"I always beat Bexley, too," Vaughn slurred out. Each day, her speaking voice was becoming progressively harder to understand. Bexley was trying to appreciate each day, because she knew the day was coming when she'd never hear her sister speak again. It was in these moments that Bexley knew nothing she was facing could ever be that bad. She needed to suck things up and put one foot in front of the other, one day at a time.

"So, what's on the agenda today?" Bexley asked as she poured some coffee into Vaughn's "Queen of Damn Near Everything" mug. It was the little things that made Bexley smile these days, and this funny, sparkly mug of Vaughn's had done the trick.

"Well, her royal highness and I were thinking of going to Central

Park today, maybe look at the gardens again before it gets too cold and they're covered in snow. Want to come?" Mary Jane asked.

Bexley looked at Vaughn and saw the forlorn look her eyes. There was no way she would disappoint her sister on this beautiful, sunny day. Who knew how many more days like this her sister would even see?

Bexley swallowed hard and put a happy face on. "Of course! Let me just go shower and I'll be right out and ready to go. Should we bring a picnic lunch?"

"Great idea, Bex," Vaughn said. "MJ can pack it." Vaughn smiled sweetly at her aide.

Bexley headed to the bathroom to get ready. She stripped off all of her clothes and stood naked in front of the full-length mirror, just looking at her body. She ran her hands along her breasts and torso. She couldn't imagine what it felt like to be Vaughn and watch her body go through all the stages of deterioration. She wondered how she would feel about her own body in the coming months. Bex shook her head, unable to think about it any further this morning.

She took her time getting ready, enjoying the sunlight that streamed into her bedroom as she put her makeup on at the silver mirrored vanity she'd purchased once in New York. It was so girly, and so unlike anything she'd ever owned before. But she was setting up roots now, and she needed her own pieces.

Her thoughts went out to Kai, suddenly sad about all he was missing, and she wondered if a phone call later was in order. They had only Skyped a handful of times. It was extremely difficult for Bexley when they did. She wasn't good at long-distance relationships, and couldn't see a solution in sight. She sighed, not letting her mind wander to the "what-ifs" right now. She would worry about those in a few months. Her immediate focus was on Vaughn.

October in New York City was not as warm as October in Laguna. Bexley slid into some skinny jeans, a long angora sweater, tall riding boots, and a scarf. She turned from side to side in the mirror. *Not too shabby*, she thought with a big grin that lit up her slightly freckled face. Sweaters would be her best friends this winter.

They made their way to Central Park, having to take a taxi van with wheelchair access. The Conservatory Garden had quickly become one of Bexley's favorites to stroll around. They walked slowly over to the South Garden, her favorite for its delicate pink Carefree Wonder Roses. She took a deep inhale of their subtle fragrance and smiled. She looked around. She knew it was against the rules, but she popped a flower head from the shrub and held it to Vaughn's nose. Park security could suck it. It was worth the potential fine just to see the wide smile that spread over Vaughn's face. The sister she remembered was in the twinkle of her eyes at that moment, and Bexley would give anything for another few memories like this. She bent down and hugged her sister.

She stood up and turned from Vaughn's wheelchair while she wiped a tear from her eye. That's when she saw him walking toward her. She shook her head, unable to process what in the world Kai was doing in New York City—in the same garden, at the same moment as they were.

"Kai? Oh my God!" Bexley squealed. She ran and jumped into his arms, wrapping her legs around his waist. She felt Kai's strong, muscular arms reach up and wrap around her, hugging her to him as if he never wanted to let her go again. She lost it then, crying into his shoulder like the hot mess that she was. He stroked her hair and whispered, "It's okay, firecracker. I'm here now."

She pulled back her head and wiped the tears from her face, then leaned down and kissed him. They stayed locked together like that, in a never-ending kiss it seemed, until they heard a gentle, "Eh-hem," from behind Bexley.

Bexley turned her head and saw Vaughn and Mary Jane watching them, smirks on their faces. "How about an introduction, sis?" Vaughn slurred out slowly.

She turned and looked into Kai's crystal blue eyes, not wanting to break free from their embrace. Three months had been far too long, and now that he was here with her again, Bexley wasn't quite sure how she had ever walked away—even if it was after only one night. But, Bexley admitted to herself, it had been the best night of her life. She looked back at Vaughn and reminded herself of *why* she had left. There's nothing she wouldn't do for her sister, even if it meant postponing her own happiness—or walking away from it.

"I'm sorry, Vaughn, Mary Jane, this"—she waved her hand in Kai's direction after sliding down out of his embrace—"is Kai. Kai, my sister Vaughn, and her aide Mary Jane."

"Nice to finally meet you," Vaughn said, smiling. "Mary Jane, let's go to the North Garden, give them some privacy?"

"Vaughn, you don't have to do that!" Bexley said, though selfishly she craved some alone time with Kai. Find out what made him travel across the country just to see her. If that was even why he was in New York. She had so many questions and so much to tell him.

"Bexley, you know she doesn't have the energy that she used to have. Here, I'll leave this picnic basket with you and take her over to the North Garden. Why don't we make our own way home, since it'll probably need to be soon. You can catch the train back, or get a cab with Kai, if you like. It was nice to meet you," Mary Jane said to Kai, then began pushing Vaughn in the opposite direction toward the North Garden.

"Hmm," said Bexley, cocking her eyebrow at Kai. "I'm starting to feel a little set up!"

"Who? Me?" Kai draped his arm around her shoulder and planted a kiss on the side of her head. "I'm just so happy to be here, to actually hold you and kiss you again. I've missed you so much, Bexley. By the way," he said, flipping a strand of her shoulder-length bob, "Love the new hairdo. Very New York. Sexy," he growled.

Bexley blushed as she looked up into his dreamy blue eyes. *I could lose myself in them forever.* But forever was a long time, and not in Bexley's vocabulary. She couldn't promise Kai any more than she could commit to in the moment. She wouldn't, not even given the news she knew she should share with him.

"Let's sit and eat, if you're hungry," Bexley said, peeking at Kai from the corner of her eyes as they walked to a nearby bench, the picnic basket in tow.

"I'm famished," Kai said and winked at Bexley. "But I guess I could eat some lunch first," he said with a straight face.

"Nice, music man." Bexley could not stop staring at him, wanting to pinch herself to see if this was real.

"Let's eat while we talk," Kai suggested, sitting near the fountain. "This place is gorgeous! I can see why it's your favorite," he said, looking around in wonder.

"Wait . . . how did you know it was my favorite?" Bexley asked.

"I may've talked to your sister before coming," Kai admitted, looking rather sheepish.

Bexley paled. "She didn't tell you anything, did she?"

Kai suddenly looked worried. "No, why? Should she have?"

"No," Bexley said, letting out a sigh of relief. "But . . . there is something I need to talk to you about. I'm glad you came out, actually. This isn't a conversation I'd want to have over Skype." Bexley looked down and took Kai's hands in her own.

It was Kai's turn to pale. Bexley had no idea what thoughts were swirling around in that gorgeous head of his, but she was almost certain it wasn't anywhere close to what she was about to say.

chapter Seventeen

"Did you really just say the word pregnant?" Kai ran a hand through his thick, dark hair and sat back, his arms around the back of the wrought iron bench. He took a long, slow breath. Then he turned to Bexley and hugged her, hard. He brought his hands to both sides of her face and kissed her, savoring the taste of her lips. "Oh my God! I'm going to be a father!"

Bexley sputtered. "Whoa, slow down, Daddy-O. *We* haven't made any decisions around this baby just yet. I cannot believe you aren't more freaked out over this. Where's the angst? You're supposed to be filled with angst and uncertainty," she huffed.

"Bexley, if you're pregnant, you're pregnant. There's no going back or wishing for something different. And, yeah, I'd like to say I'm completely surprised, but I'm not really. I mean, we didn't use any protection the night we were together. I've never done that before," Kai admitted. "But what do you want me to say? I'm *not* unhappy with the result."

Bexley stared at Kai, her mouth hanging open in disbelief. She shook her head and then turned away, lowering her face in her hands. "I just don't need this right now, Kai. It's awful timing. My sister is dying. I mean, did you *see* her? They have no idea how long she has left, but I can feel in my heart that it's not long. She needs twenty-four-hour care and supervision. I'm running a new business basically all by myself here. And I have no fucking clue what I am going to do when she passes. And now I'm supposed to be happy to be throwing a baby into the mix? No. Just no."

Kai looked away. He understood where she was coming from, but he was secretly overjoyed. A baby. With Bexley. His heart did somersaults. He couldn't wait to tell his cousin Josh.

Kai didn't want to pin Bexley down this way, but he was so happy for the unexpected news. It did not freak him out in the slightest. In fact, he believed if they stuck together and acted as a team on this, they could get through anything.

"Look, I know you're scared, Bexley—"

"Please do not even say what I think you're going to say," she said through gritted teeth.

"And what exactly did you think I was going to say, smarty pants?" he asked. His arms were crossed over his chest, but a smile of amusement rode his cheeks, bringing out his dimple.

"That I can't run away forever. I have to face some things head on."

"Well, that is true, Bex. But it wasn't what I was going to say. I was just going to say that I know you are fiercely independent and used to having to handle everything on your own. But this is my baby too. And you don't have to figure out all of the tough life decisions on your own anymore. I want to be here for you, Bex. Like, all the time. Just let me in, okay? We can do this. We can get through anything, if you just trust me. Let me stick."

His eyes searched Bexley's, looking for any clue that she was on the same page as he was. "Does Vaughn know? Is that why she called me? How did you even find out?"

Bexley took a deep breath, her hands visibly shaking in her lap. "Well, I've been running myself too ragged lately, taking on too much with learning the new business during the day and taking care of Vaughn at night. I really need to get a night nurse from here on out. I'll still be worried, but maybe I'll actually get some sleep." Bexley glanced over at the roses and took a sip of the water that Kai handed to her from the picnic basket. "Thanks," she said gratefully, taking a huge swallow from the glass bottle.

"I guess I haven't been very careful about making sure I eat all the time, and was getting anemic without realizing it. Coupled with the pregnancy I knew nothing about, I think my body just collapsed as Vaughn and I were talking about a pretty heavy topic in the office. She had to call 911." Bexley chewed the inside of her mouth. "I hate that I gave her something more to worry about."

"Maybe it'll be something she'll be excited about and look forward to. Maybe it will help her hold on longer?" Kai offered.

Bexley nodded, but said nothing for a few moments. "I don't know if I even want this baby, Kai. I mean"—she put her hands over her flat stomach, as if searching for the answers there—"it just doesn't feel real yet. We were only together *one* night, Kai. What do you have? Superhero swimmers?"

Kai burst out laughing. "Oh, baby, you know I do," he teased, winking at her playfully. "Bex . . . it only takes once. Though, I think technically it was four or five times," Kai said, smiling sheepishly.

"I know you're still processing all of this, and I am too. It's your body and I'll respect any decision you make with it in the end. But if I get a vote, I vote for the baby. I vote for us. Give us a chance, Bexley. I was serious when I said I would come out here and help support you. I know in my heart that everything happens for a reason. This baby was no mistake. Whether you like it or not, you're going to be my family now. We're going to be connected for the rest of our lives through this little miracle we created."

Kai reached out and rubbed Bexley's flat tummy. "Hi, little

juju bean," he whispered. He was totally enamored already and they didn't even know the baby's gender. "How far along are you?" he asked. Then smacked himself on the forehead. "Duh. Three months, one week, four days."

"You've been counting?" Bexley asked, surprised.

"I've missed you every day, Bexley, wondering when we would be able to see each other again in person. I didn't want to push you, because of the stress you're under with your sister and the new life you're building. But I had no intention of ever giving up on you. You had me at 'Take a picture, it'll last longer,'" Kai said, laughing. "Knew right from that moment you were going to be my little firecracker. And you did not disappoint."

Bexley blushed and looked down at her hands that were folded in her lap. "There are just so many decisions we'll need to iron out. I don't know how to make all of this work. We don't even really know each other very well, and now we're going to—what? Have a baby together? Merge our lives? I don't know how to do any of this, Kai. You live across the country for God's sake!"

"I don't either, Bex. I've never had a baby before. I've never lived with someone before—"

"Whoa. Back up, music man. Who said you're living with me?"

"Bexley . . . eventually I'll need to, to help you take care of the baby. Who's going to watch it when you're working all day, taking care of your sister's business? I can stay home with our baby during the day so we don't have to pay for childcare. I'm sure it's crazy expensive in New York. But I can give music lessons at night or on the weekends to help supplement our income and give us a little wiggle room."

Bexley just stared at Kai. "You seem to have this all figured out for just finding out. Are you sure Vaughn didn't spill the beans earlier?"

"It just makes sense, Bexley. Let me into your life. We can do this if we face it together." He leaned in and cupped her face, taking her lips in his own and sealing the deal with a kiss that left him breathless, and even more head over heels in love with her. "God, Bex . . . I have missed you so much. Are you feeling better now?" he asked, wiggling his brows.

"Yes, I think I'm back to normal," she said, hedging. "Why, what's going on in that little brain of yours?"

"Baby, nothing on me is little." Kai laughed, then took her hand, stroking it slowly with his thumb. "I have a hotel room all to myself. Why don't we go back and put it to good use? I want to see you, and hold you. I've been thinking about you every day since you left, Bexley. It's torture to be this close to you and not have my hands all over your skin yet. Will you come back to the hotel with me?" he asked, praying she would say yes. Yes to the baby. Yes to their future. And yes to a little afternoon romp.

Bexley didn't think she'd have the energy for a full-out, tear-your-clothes-off romp in the sack after what she'd just been through the day before. But when they closed the hotel room door, something broke down Bexley's defenses and she caved. She looked at Kai, all raw and honest, opening his heart to her in a way she never expected given the bomb she'd just dropped on him. She looked around at the half-unpacked suitcase, his guitar resting in a club chair, his manscaping products jumbled all over the small bathroom counter. The coffee pot was half full, and Bexley suddenly gasped.

"What's wrong?" Kai asked, worried.

Bexley looked up at the concern on Kai's face and laughed. "Sorry . . . it just dawned on me that I won't be able to have any coffee for the next six months. What the fuck am I going to do?"

Kai burst out laughing. "Babe, no worries. I'll give you all the energy you need each day. And then some," he said, wrapping his hands around her waist and pulling her closer. He rested his forehead on hers and inhaled deeply. "Ah . . . I'm so glad that you still smell like oranges. I was afraid it was just a California thing. You smell exactly how I remember you—sweet and edible."

Bexley shivered when Kai bent his head and kissed the inside crook of her neck. It sent waves of heat straight to her belly, but she squirmed under the touch of his lips, gasping in a fit of giggles.

"Ooh—how did I not realize this was your ticklish spot?" he teased. He ran his tongue up her neck and nibbled her shoulder slowly.

Bexley leaned her head back and opened her neck up farther to him, enjoying the feel of his lips caressing her skin. She wasn't sure if it was the pregnancy hormones running through her or the fact that she'd gone over three months without sex, but damn! Every nerve ending in her body felt alive, hyper energized. She laughed. "My own secret energy shot: vitamin K. I think I need a large dose today, music man."

He moved his guitar from the club chair and pulled it in front of the big window overlooking the city. They were really high up and only a few buildings had a line of sight into Kai's room. He took her hand and led her to the chair, pointing to it. "Sit."

"Ooh, I kinda like this bossy, take-charge Kai."

"Oh, I'll show you bossy, firecracker." He pulled his shirt up over his head and lowered his jeans. He was wearing boxers today, and Bexley couldn't wait to take them off for him. Kai made eye contact and sauntered over to the chair where Bexley was waiting, getting wetter by the second. There was something so sexy and masculine about the way Kai carried himself. Something she never would have expected from a middle school music teacher.

"Damn . . . those girls in your class probably have wet dreams every night about their music teacher," Bexley said and laughed. "Mr. Donovan, I've been very naughty and have been sticking gum under my desk. Do you think maybe I ought to be punished?" Bexley batted her eyelashes at Kai for good measure.

Kai's half-grin sent shivers down to her toes, excited at how he might "discipline" her. He picked Bexley up out of the chair and folded her over across his lap as he sat down.

He rubbed his hand over her plump cheek, squeezing it and kneading it. "So juicy," he said. "Just like a California orange. I think I may need to take a bite . . . but first, your discipline." He pulled his hand back and smacked her bottom. Hard. Her cheek smarted, but the pain was delicious. She raised her rump in the air, wiggling it suggestively. He kneaded it again, but didn't spank her a second time. Instead, he lifted her up and asked her to stand.

Kai lifted her angora sweater up over the top of her jeans, drawing her closer to him in the process. His warm mouth met her stomach and he began kissing the soft, delicate skin near her belly button. Bexley remembered all of the amazing things Kai could do with his tongue, and she moaned as he plunged it into her belly button, soft and wet. Roughly, he unzipped her jeans and slid them down her legs, pulling off her boots so he could get the pants off, too. Then he stood, lifting her sweater above her head and seeing her matching bra and panty set for the first time. Bright candy apple red, and lace. Lots of lace and skin. She hadn't known she was going to see Kai today, but she was so happy she took the time to dress from H-to-T today.

Kai sat back down and pulled Bexley into his lap again, this time so that she was almost facing him. She leaned her head down and kissed his lips softly at first, wanting so badly to feel him against her, take in the whole of him. He kissed her back with the patience of a saint. Oh, it was hot; the agonizingly slow and patient kind of hot. But Bexley was in the mood for fast and explosive. She ran her hands up and down his chest, fingering the top of his boxer shorts.

"Uh-uh," Kai said. "I'm not done disciplining you yet, Miss Rue." He spun her around and had her back on her stomach before she could respond. Heat went straight to her belly in anticipation. "God, your skin is so soft," he said as the flat of his palm rubbed the smooth skin of her ass. He leaned over and took some of her flesh into his mouth, sucking hard. He ran his hand up and down her opening, where her legs came together. He pulled the material of her thong to the side, slowly running his fingers along her warm center. God, she was so freaking wet for him already.

Whack! It took Bexley's breath away when the second smack on her bottom came. It wasn't too hard, but it felt like liquid lust, right between her legs. She felt his fingers slide slowly inside of her. They slid smoothly, back and forth, and she couldn't help but lift her bottom and press it against his hand, riding it as he deftly played her as if she were the strings of his guitar.

Then emptiness.

Smack!

He rubbed his hand over the spot on her ass that he'd been spanking. Bexley knew she would be red there, and the thought made her tingle even more.

Kai stood up and set Bexley down onto the chair, facing him. "Your punishment is over, Miss Rue. Now, I think it's time for a little Sex Ed."

He pulled her hips forward so she was nearly at the end of the cushion. He lowered her red panties down over her knees and to the floor. Kai sat on his shins as he bent down, stroking the outside of her lips, slowly, excruciatingly so. He leaned over and blew onto her wetness, reaching his tongue out and flickering it once. It shot jolts of lightning to Bexley's tummy at the anticipation of feeling his warm tongue on her. "God yes, Kai," she said. "I want to feel your mouth on me."

"What else, Miss Rue? What would make you come for me?" he teased, running his fingers along the outsides of her folds while kissing her inner thighs and causing her to squirm in the sweetest, most agonizing way.

"I want to feel your fingers inside of me. I want to ride your hand until I come. I want you to fuck me with your tongue. Is that enough direction, teacher?"

"Oh, you're a firecracker, all right. How's this?" he asked, plunging three fingers deep inside of Bexley until he could go no farther. He pulled them back and plunged them in again, over and over as she rode his hand. He crooked his fingers inside of her wetness and put pressure with his other hand just above her mons. Bexley started to come from all of the delicious attention to her G-spot. "God, Kai. Yes!"

He removed his fingers as her orgasm slowed and bent his head to lick her. She put her fingers right into that thick hair of his, exactly as she'd done on the kitchen counter in Laguna. Kai ran his tongue up and down along the outside of her lips, licking up the sweet juices she'd just released. Her legs shook around his head as she continued to come down from her orgasmic high. Her head fell against the chair's back as she closed her eyes, her fingers gently playing with Kai's hair in pure bliss. She sighed.

"I guess you liked that lesson plan, then?" Kai teased.

Bexley murmured, half sleepily, "Oh, man. Did I ever." She opened her eyes and could see the New York sky, a dusky blue with tufts of white clouds billowed throughout. *Under the same sky.* Bexley closed her eyes again, and took a jagged breath in.

Kai lifted Bexley from the chair and brought her to the bed. He swiped off the extra clothes he'd tossed on there earlier and made room to lie Bexley down. She lifted her arms above her head and stretched like a sexy, satiated cat. "Mmm," she said. "Come here so I can teach you a thing or two."

Kai reached his hand over and rubbed her hair. She was getting so sleepy and she didn't know why. But Kai must have understood because he curled up around her and they lay there, spooning until all thoughts were gone from Bexley's mind except the soft, comfortable sounds of Kai sleeping.

chapter Eighteen

Bexley awoke in a panic when she realized how dark it was outside. "Vaughn!" she said, throwing her legs over the side of the bed.

Kai crossed the room and put his hands on her legs, squatting in front of her so they were face to face. "Shh," he said. "It's okay. I already worked it out with Mary Jane. She's going to spend the night with Vaughn so we can have some more time together to work things out."

Bexley ran a hand through her tousled hair. "How long have I been asleep?" She looked around the hotel room and noticed the picnic basket on the floor. Her stomach rumbled and she realized they never really ate lunch. "Is there anything in there that hasn't spoiled? I'm famished."

Kai laughed. "Doesn't surprise me. It's after eight."

"Eight? Why did you let me sleep so long?" She yawned and stretched, trying to shake the sleep from her system.

"Exactly," he said, with a pointed brow. He got up and brought the picnic basket over to the bed, setting it down next to Bexley. He rubbed her back as she riffled through it, searching for non-perishables.

Damn! Most everything had been finger foods and salads, and they didn't look too appetizing anymore. She found a mini baguette and pulled it out. She wasn't usually a carbs girl, but she tore it in half and bit in. "Mmm," she said, letting her eyes close as the fresh bread melted against her tongue. *Okay, maybe I've been too harsh on carbs.*

She sighed. When she opened her eyes, Kai was sitting at the small desk, his laptop open.

"So, what have you been up to these last few hours while I've been snoozing over here?" Her eyes widened. "Oh my gosh! I didn't snore, did I? Please tell me I didn't snore."

"Why? Do you usually?" Kai asked, an amused grin splitting his handsome face. Bexley adored the five o'clock shadow that brushed his jawline.

"Of course not!" Bexley sputtered. "But, you know, sometimes when I'm really tired . . ." She shrugged and took another bite of her bread. "Have anymore bottled water lying around anywhere?" she asked, looking around the small space.

He handed her one of the complimentary bottles that was on the desk. Bexley leaned over and tried to see what he was working on all this time. Kai quickly closed the laptop.

"Hey! I was snooping, you know!"

"Exactly!" Kai said again and laughed.

"You're not even here twenty-four hours and you're already hiding things from me?" she asked, miffed. She pouted for good measure.

"Bex, I'd never hide anything from you. But maybe I'd like to have a few mysteries about myself, so you don't get bored with me too quickly."

"Just know that I hate surprises," Bexley warned. She didn't like the way Kai squirmed when she said that. *Uh-oh.*

"Kai, what's going on?"

"Well, oh impatient one, I *was* going to surprise you, but I wasn't going to keep it a secret or anything. I actually started doing some research about how to transfer my teaching license. And I may've put in my notice at work already. Oh, and—"

"Whoa, back up. Did you just say you quit your job?"

Kai's face reddened. "I might have."

"Kai! Why would you do that? We haven't even agreed if I'm keeping this baby yet." The words flew out of her mouth before she could stop them, but Bexley wished she could take them back the instant she watched Kai's face fall, as if someone had just told him he'd lost his best friend.

He put his hands on his knees and lowered his head between his legs, taking long, deep breaths. Bexley was afraid to say anything, afraid of making things worse. But it was the truth. She didn't know if she could raise this baby. She couldn't see past Vaughn's immediate needs, let alone a year from now. That wasn't her. She hated planning, and being responsible, and—oh, fuck.

A baby. She was going to have a real live actual little human being.

Bexley started hyperventilating.

Kai rushed over and sat next to her, his warm hand running soft circles on her back. "Bex, I know you've gotten used to going full throttle with everything since coming to New York. And I know Vaughn wants her business to succeed and is relying on you. But things are different now. Whether you like it or not, you are carrying my baby. I want to make these decisions together. But I think maybe you need to pull back a little and slow down." He raked his hand through his hair. Bexley sat there looking at his handsome face, wishing she could reach out to him. Let him all the way in. She knew he was trying.

"You need to slow down, Bexley. Whether you like it or not, it's not just you that you have to worry about anymore."

Bexley stopped cold, straightening her back and clenching her jaw. "Not just me? Are you fucking kidding me, Kai? The whole reason I'm here in New York is because I can't just think of me anymore."

Bexley stood, anger blinding her vision. *I have to get out of here.* She started grabbing her clothes from the floor, throwing pieces on haphazardly.

"Bex, stop. That is not what I meant—"

She leveled Kai with her gaze. She threw the red thong she was holding in her hands into the trash can, too angry to put them on now that her jeans were already zipped up. She missed and they dangled there on the ledge, half in, half out. *Like me*, Bex thought.

She groaned. "You know what, Kai? It doesn't matter what you meant. You said it. Yes, I'm selfish. I've always been selfish. It's what I love about not being pinned down. I guess I am truly a gypsy soul after all. I don't know how to think of anyone but myself because I've never had to, Kai. How the fuck can I take care of a baby when I can't even take care of myself?" She threw her arms in the air, exasperated. "I can't even keep Vaughn alive, Kai. How will I raise a baby?"

"Bexley, calm down. It's completely different and you know it. And I didn't mean that the way it sounded. I just meant that you need to slow down. You're going to need to take better care of yourself now, not just Vaughn. That's why I want to be here. Because you're right. You can't do it on your own. Fuck, Bex. No one could. You only have twenty-four hours in a day, and you have three lives and a business to care for now. Let me help, damn it!"

They both stood there, taking large, deep breaths, seething in their own indignation about the situation they'd found themselves in. Bexley was the one who broke the silence.

"I can't do this, Kai. Not right now. I need time to think. I need space."

"Bex, we've had three months of space. Do you really want to do this?" Kai put his hands on his hips and frowned.

Bexley knew she wasn't being fair, but she just needed to get out of the small hotel room. It was closing in on her.

"It's what I do best, Kai," she said, sadly. She grabbed the picnic basket off the bed and headed toward the door. Bexley knew she was making the biggest mistake of her life, but she was broken and tired and confused. She had nowhere left to turn.

So she headed home to her dying sister, looking for answers she wasn't ready to hear.

chapter Nineteen

By the time Bexley got back to her apartment, Vaughn was asleep. She found Mary Jane curled up on the sofa in the open loft space, reading *Until I Say Good-Bye*. Bexley had seen the book lying around, but she hadn't been able to pick it up yet.

"Hey, MJ," Bexley said, setting the picnic basket on the kitchen counter. "How is she?"

"The question isn't how is Vaughn, it's how are you? You weren't supposed to be back tonight, child." Mary Jane set her book down and frowned when she saw Bexley's face. "Girl, what happened? You look like you just lost your best friend or something."

Bexley thought back to the look on Kai's face when she

admitted she wasn't sure if she wanted to keep the baby or not. Her heart ached. *What have I done?*

Bexley flopped onto the sofa next to Mary Jane. She put her head in her hands and started to cry. Ugly cry. Big, heaving, wracking spasms.

Mary Jane put her arm around Bexley and held her, stroking her hair and whispering that it would be all right. Bexley fell into the comfort of the older woman's arms. It had been a long time since she'd felt any compassion from a mother figure. Which only made Bexley's tears fall even faster, her body shaking with each gasp for air.

She sat up, looking around the living room for a tissue. Mary Jane handed her the cylinder of Puffs, and Bexley gratefully wiped her eyes and blew her nose. "Oh, man, MJ. I'm a complete wreck tonight."

"Pregnancy hormones will do that to a girl," Mary Jane said.

"Oh great. So on top of everything else, I'm going to be a walking hormonal mess?" Bexley looked at Mary Jane, whose eyebrow was arched in amusement. "Okay, I mean an even bigger walking hormonal mess?" Bexley let out a shaky laugh. "Christ in a bucket, we're all in trouble."

"Sweetie, my momma told me when I was expecting my first child that there would be so many highs and lows I'd lose count. But that the minute I laid eyes on my little one, all the lows would be forgotten. And she was right. The instant I first saw my

Rosaleigh, it was love at first sight. Strongest bond I've ever felt. Scared the life right out of me, how she would look at me with those wise old eyes of hers. On a baby, too! Like she could see right through to my very insides. I couldn't hide anymore once I had Rosaleigh. Made me come forward in life in a way I'd never had to before."

"How old were you when you had her?" Bexley asked.

"Girl, you might as well be asking how old I am now," Mary Jane said and laughed. She fluffed her graying brown curls primly. "But it's okay. I was twenty-one when I had her. And I had her all alone. So it was just me and her, growing up together."

Bexley looked at Mary Jane in a new light. So often, she'd just seen her as an extra set of hands to help her sister. "How did you do it? Raising her all by yourself? It scares the bejesus right out of me."

"There's a difference, though, between us, Bex. I didn't have a choice. You do."

"What do you mean?"

"I didn't know Rosaleigh's daddy, Bex. She wasn't my choice, if you catch my meaning. But you know what? God has bigger plans for us than we can ever dream for ourselves. He knows what we need even before we do. And you know what?"

Mary Jane paused as Bexley bit her lower lip, afraid of what God was offering her. Afraid to take it in her hands and trust it.

"Rosaleigh was *never* a mistake. And your little one? A beautiful blessing right there, too. So whether Kai steps in and helps you or not, don't you give up on that little angel you got in there. You hear me? The truth is, Vaughn isn't going to make it much longer. I can see it in her eyes, Bexley. Now, I know you don't want to hear this," MJ said, placing a hand on top of Bexley's, "but she needs you to be strong. She needs to talk to you about her end of life plans before she can't voice them anymore. And she wants you to be happy, Bexley. After she's gone. I think God knew exactly what he was doing, giving you this unexpected little miracle."

Mary Jane got up off the sofa and tucked the book under her arm. "I'm plum tuckered out after today. Had a hard time getting Vaughn to eat anything. She's choking on her food more and more now. Had to give the poor girl a protein shake for dinner. Think we're gonna need the feeding tube next week, Bexley."

"Already?" Bexley whispered, shaking her head no.

"Yeah, baby. Already." Mary Jane leaned over and hugged Bexley. "I know it's a whole hell of a lot, beautiful girl. But here's my advice: let Kai help. If you love him as much as Vaughn thinks you do, let the poor man help. You're gonna need it. Not just for the physical support, but your heart's gonna need a place to call home, too."

Bexley nodded, squeezing MJ's hand before the aide went back to Vaughn's room for the night. She looked at the clock. It was only ten p.m., but Bexley couldn't remember ever feeling so bone tired in her whole life. She would sleep on it. Her head and her heart had had enough for the day. Too many highs and too many lows. She went to bed with prayers on her lips that tomorrow she'd forget the lows and be able to move forward with a focus on the highs in her life. That night, she fell asleep hopeful for the first time in months, her hand gently hugging the tiny curve of her stomach as she drifted off.

"Bexley Rue! Please tell me you did not come home last night," she heard before she even cracked open her eyes.

"Ugh, nmphrfle," Bexley moaned into her pillow. "What time is it?" she asked, peering from under her lightweight duvet. It was gray and cloudy outside; tiny raindrops hit the sole window with their diagonal precision.

Vaughn sat in her wheelchair at the entrance to Bexley's bedroom, Mary Jane standing discreetly off to the side. "It's time to grow up, that's what time it is," Vaughn said. Bexley knew that if it had been the old Vaughn, she would've flipped her hair haughtily over her shoulder and stormed out of the room.

Guilt washed over Bexley, forcing her to sit up and face the day. "Look, it was a really long night, and my heart is a little bruised right now, so please don't start in on me before I've had my coffee," Bexley grumbled.

Vaughn cleared her throat and Mary Jane stepped forward, handing Bexley a steaming mug of her favorite vanilla latte. She took a long swallow before remembering she shouldn't really be drinking coffee anymore. Guilt oozed down her throat like the overly sweet concoction she'd just sipped. Both were hard to swallow. She handed the mug back to Mary Jane.

"It's time, Bexley. I'll meet you in fifteen minutes in the living room. You and I need to chat. Sorry if it's not good timing, but there are a few things I need to tell you before I can't anymore. So, today's the day, buttercup."

Mary Jane smiled weakly at Bexley before pulling Vaughn's wheelchair back and maneuvering it down the hall toward the living room.

Bexley sighed, picking up her phone and turning it on. There was one SnapChat of the gray, cloudy skyline from Kai's hotel room window. On it, he'd written: "Under the same sky." Bexley smiled. *Damn him.*

She pulled on some yoga pants and an ALS Sucks sweatshirt and padded into the living room. She'd set her coffee down onto an end table and was twisting her hair into a messy topknot when she paused, mid-twirl. Scattered all over the coffee table were photographs. Bexley swallowed hard and stepped closer, peering over the edge of the couch as she finished securing her hair. *I will not cry.*

"What's all this?" she asked, trying to sound casual. She walked slowly around the sofa until she was in front of the coffee table. There were dozens of old photographs, mostly black and white, because that was her father's favorite. Bexley's heart felt as if it was going to break in two. But she'd run from Vaughn long enough, and she owed her this. Owed it to hear her sister out, while she could.

"Your sister and I found these old photographs a few weeks ago, while we were planning Vaughn's funeral service." Mary Jane held up her hand and shushed Bexley when she saw that she was about to interrupt. "Come on now, Bexley. You know she wants to plan everything herself. She specifically asked me to put some old family pictures in a slide show I'm making for her. We found these gems in a box of your parents belongings that she'd put away."

"Exactly when were you going to tell me all of this, Vaughn?"

"Sweetie, I've been trying. You've been running the other way for weeks now. Looks like life made the decision for us, huh?" Vaughn said, an awkward smile trying to form for Bexley.

"What do you mean, Vaughn?" Bexley asked.

"I mean Kai. I mean your pregnancy. I mean all of this—" she paused and looked over at Mary Jane. "MJ, come sweep my hand around like I'm making a big gesture," Vaughn said, totally serious.

Mary Jane lifted Vaughn's hand and swept it from left to right, as if gesturing the whole of their space. "Thanks," Vaughn whispered. "I had to make a point."

Bexley grinned at her sister. God, she loved that girl. Tears started to build up, and she choked them back as well as she could.

"I'm dying, Bex. We've known that. It hurts to talk. I can hardly swallow. Fuck. I can't even hold my damn head up straight anymore."

"Then let's not talk," Bexley said. "We don't need to do this. Mary Jane can tell me what your wishes are. Don't hurt yourself, Vaughn."

"I need to, Bex. Don't you get it? Everything is being taken from me," she said and coughed, choking on something Bexley couldn't see. "Give me this," she rasped.

"Okay," Bexley sighed. "Okay. I'm sorry, Vaughn. I'm so sorry."

"Stop. You're not allowed to cry yet. Tell me what happened with Kai. Why'd you come home?"

Mary Jane adjusted the pillow behind Vaughn's head as Bexley stared off across the room, her eyes unfocused on the present, but her heart recalling her stupid words and actions from the night before.

"I fucked up, Vaughn. He took the news like a champ. More than a champ. He's willing to throw his own life away to move across the country and take care of me and our . . . our baby. God, Vaughn. How can I take care of a baby? I'm holding on by my fingernails as it is with the business and with—"

Bexley stopped. Ashamed.

"With me?" Vaughn said. "It's okay, Bex. It's okay to admit how hard it all is. I didn't mean to dump all of this on you. I didn't think I'd die so soon. But I know he loves you, and—"

"What did you just say?" Bexley asked, her mouth hanging open.

"What part? Oh, the 'he loves you' part. I should've known it would freak you out."

"He doesn't love me, Vaughn. It's too soon for that."

"Tell his heart that, dummy."

Bexley swallowed, looking between MJ and Vaughn.

"Mm-hmm," said Mary Jane. "Boy's head over heels, Bexley. I told you so last night."

Vaughn coughed again, trying to clear her throat. "He wants this to work, Bex. He isn't throwing away his life for you. He's choosing a better one with you. Don't you get that? You've always been running away from something, Bexley. Well, he's running *toward* something. And that something is a life with you. Stand tall and stick around this time, Bexley. For him. For that baby growing inside of you."

"I don't know how to stick, Vaughn! That's the problem. He's asking me to love him, to let him just waltz into our lives, and I don't know how to let him in. I have spent my whole life running from love, avoiding getting too close because I knew it wouldn't last, that I wouldn't stay. I've never truly, deep down loved a man before. Let alone a baby. I don't even know if I can." Bexley dropped her head into her hands and let the tears fall.

"Vaughn, it just hurts too freaking much when they leave you. When they die. I'm not sure I can open my heart like that and let it get shattered again. Jesus, it's about to get decimated into a million pieces when I lose you. How can I risk letting Kai in too?"

Vaughn dropped her eyes to her lap and sighed. "Bex, there's so much you don't know. I need to tell you something."

Bexley shook her head, even as Vaughn was trying unsuccessfully to nod hers. "Yes. We have to face this together, so I know you have a shot at happiness after I'm gone. Promise me that. Don't use my death as an excuse to not allow yourself to open up to Kai—to the family he wants to create with you. He loves you, Bexley. I could see it in how he looks at you, how he worried about you. You deserve that kind of love."

"But what happens in a year when I get scared and want to run? Follow my gypsy heart again? What then?"

"Bexley, drop it with the gypsy heart. You can't keep using that to excuse yourself from getting close to another human being. There's something you need to know, and I need you to listen to all of it. Promise me?"

Bexley had never seen her sister get so stern with her. Even though she was the older sister, structured and disciplined, she'd always worn soft, protective gloves with Bexley. More like a second mother than a sister.

"Okay, I promise. Now what is it? You're freaking me out a little."

Vaughn took a deep breath, though she looked like she was struggling. Her eyes were among the few things left that could still fully express her emotions to others. She met Bexley's gaze, her eyes never wavering. "Before Mom and Dad died, when I was in college and you were still in high school, I confronted Mom about some things. So she asked if she could confide in me. She was really nervous, twisting her hands and such. But she had to get something off her chest, so I let her."

"What did she say?" Bexley asked, inching toward the edge of the sofa.

"She admitted that she had had a longtime lover before Dad."

Bexley gasped. "What? I thought they were childhood sweethearts? When did she—were they married?"

"No. Though at one point, she wanted to marry him. They had a child together, and she was very much in love."

"What did you just say?" Bexley's eyes grew round, her throat constricting. "We have a sibling somewhere? Do you know who it is?"

Vaughn glanced quickly at Mary Jane and swallowed. "Yeah, I know who it is, Bexley. The baby they had together was me."

Bexley's eyes whipped up to look at her sister. "What? No . . . then that means . . ."

"It means we are sisters, Bexley. It just means we have different biological fathers."

Bexley couldn't speak for a few minutes. She picked at her fingernail, tearing the earthy Nomad's Dream color from the bed, watching it flake in little pieces and fall to the floor. "Do you—do you remember your father at all?" She couldn't even begin to reconcile any of this in her heart yet.

"No. I was too young when Mom left him."

"Why did she leave him?" Bexley choked out. She could not imagine her mother loving anyone other than their father.

"He was a police officer. She believed he was suffering from PTSD after a horrific serial murder case he had worked for several years. Back then, they didn't really know much about PTSD. He just wasn't himself after immersing himself into the brutal crimes he was tracking down. Mom said he'd been a good man before that. But he couldn't shake the things he'd seen. He became different. Angrier. Unable to control his outbursts around her. She said everything made him upset. When I cried, when she wasn't in the mood to sleep with him, if there were dirty dishes in the sink. Every little thing set him off."

"So she left him?"

"Yes, she left him. But not until he nearly beat her to death. Then she knew she had to get out to keep me safe. But he kept chasing after her, trying to find her. She went back to her hometown to get some of her things and borrow money from her parents so that she could move somewhere fresh, far away from him, and start a new life. When she was back home, she reconnected with Dad. You're right, he had been her high school sweetheart."

"Wow! How come I never knew all of this? So, did they run away together then?"

"Yes, they ran. They went to Arizona and set up a new life together. But she kept getting threatening messages from my biological father. So they had to move again. They had you in Washington state. But that didn't last long. They moved all over the West Coast, about once a year, until they felt like they were safe again. But he always seemed to track us down."

"Why didn't they just go to the police?"

"Bex, he *was* the police. Mom contacted them once, before she left him, and they blew off the complaint. Like I said, it was before they really understood PTSD outside of a war zone, and he'd been a good man, a good cop. They just couldn't believe the nice, affable man they knew at the precinct was the same man Mom was describing at home. I guess he kept all of his explosive anger in check during the day, but then let Mom and me have it at night when he got home."

"But you were just a baby!" Bexley yelled, shaking at the thought of someone hurting her innocent mother and sister. Her hand went to her stomach, rubbing it protectively.

"That's what drove Mom to finally leave him. Apparently,

something pretty bad happened. She wouldn't tell me exactly what. But it scared her enough that she packed up a bag or two and left town one evening while he was pulling an all-nighter."

"But she could never really get away," Bexley whispered. "She lived in fear all those years and we never even knew."

"Well, I began to suspect something wasn't right. Like how she avoided certain people or situations. She always seemed jumpy and nervous—if you remember, she was a chain smoker. She never took the same way home. Things like that. I think by the time I confronted her, she was just tired of running. She needed to tell someone else."

"But why didn't she want to tell me?"

"You were still in high school. She was trying to protect you, sis. That's all."

"Oh my God! Was he the one who killed them? Did he somehow make their plane go down?" Bexley asked in horror, her hand going to her stomach again.

"No, it was nothing like that. He was already dead by then. They were keeping tabs on him, too, and he died about six months before the plane accident happened. That's why Mom finally felt free to go with Dad to his conference." Vaughn let out an odd chuckle, a little slurred, a little manic. "Only about five to ten percent of all ALS cases are familial. Looks like I drew the short straw."

Bexley's hand shot to her mouth, covering it in disbelief. "No,

Vaughn. Oh my God, no." She went over and sat next to Vaughn's wheelchair, hugging her sister's lap as she sobbed on the floor next to her. She sat up, looking into Vaughn's pretty blue eyes. Now she knew why they looked so different.

"So they lived in fear because of that bastard for years. Is that why—is that why we moved so much? Solely because of him?"

"Yes," Vaughn whispered.

Bexley stood up and screamed at the top of her lungs. Then she paced the room, seething.

"Why? Why are you telling me all of this now? Did I really need to know? That you're not even my full sister? What good does it do, Vaughn?"

"Bexley, you had to know, okay? First of all, Mom and Dad made me promise that someday, after they were gone, I would tell you. And I would have, eventually. But now, everything is different. I'll be dead by this time next year—"

"No!" Bexley covered her ears. "Stop! Just stop."

"I can't, Bexley!" Vaughn said hoarsely, in as near of a scream as she could muster.

Bexley stopped her childish outburst and looked over at her sister. Sunken eyes. Skinny, lifeless arms. Propped up in a wheelchair with a headrest, her legs unmoving. *Jesus Christ, I'm selfish.*

"I'm sorry, Vaughn. I'm so sorry." She went to her sister and kneeled down, resting her head in her sister's lap again. She took her sister's hand in her own and held it as she cried. She looked up at Vaughn and said, "Tell me whatever is left. I promise I'll stop being so selfish and listen."

Vaughn nodded as well as she could, but took a few minutes to answer. "I had to tell you before I couldn't speak anymore. MJ knows everything, too, in case you have questions someday. But I need you to understand something, Bex. Dad was not a gypsy soul by choice. Yes, he pretended that's what it was. But he wasn't. He was someone who stuck. He stuck by Mom's side, despite all the trouble she brought into their relationship. There was nothing he wouldn't do for her, nowhere he wouldn't go to keep us safe. That's what all of our moves were about. Safety. Protection. Love. Not chasing some distant dream, not being flighty or irresponsible, not some romantic notion of living wild and free."

Bexley sat on the floor, crossing her ankles and resting her back against the coffee table. Her entire world view was just flipped upside down on its head, and she wasn't sure how to process all of it.

"Bex, it's okay to have a carefree soul and to love the feeling of adventure and freedom. I'm not saying that the way you live is wrong. I'm just saying not to hold onto that notion out of some misguided love for Dad's memory. He only bounced around because of his love for Mom and us. He loved fiercely and unconditionally. If you want Kai in your life, he's the kind of guy who's like Dad. I don't think there's a thing that he wouldn't do for you—or the baby you're carrying. He doesn't seem like the kind of guy who cares where he lives, as long as it makes *you* happy. You can have both, Bexley. That's all. You can have both."

Bexley let her sister's words sink in and knew she was right. She could have both. If she would only let go of the fear and crack her heart open wide enough to let Kai all the way in, fully, forever. Bexley rested her hands on her belly protectively. Somehow, in the course of just one day, she'd slipped into love with the little juju bean inside of her. She knew the same thing had happened with Kai, and it was time to face her biggest fears and finally let love all the way in.

chapter Twenty

Bexley spent the next hour cleaning the condo for Vaughn. After looking through all the old photos with her sister and reliving their past, she needed an outlet to release all of her pent up fear and uncertainty about her future. She took it out on the hardwood floors and the sleek granite countertops, scrubbing until her fingers were nearly raw. She had her earbuds in and was listening to the playlist Kai had made for her, causing her to scrub away at the already clean floors even harder.

Bexley had so many questions running through her head, and they all pointed to one answer. She wanted to go talk to Kai, but she needed to sort through some things first, figure out how to make everything okay. And she couldn't think clearly when she was around him. The damn man just muddled her common sense and made her want to believe in something that she was so terribly afraid to slip into: an easy life together.

A chime broke through her musings and she was relieved for the interruption. She looked down at her phone and saw a new text alert from Kai.

Hey, firecracker. Miss you. Saved a new song on our playlist. Listen today? Music Man

A smile spread across Bexley's face. *Damn him.* He was relentless.

She took off her gloves and set the scrubbing brush back in the bucket. She blew out a breath and lifted her bangs in the process, nervous laughter escaping her lips. Bexley perched herself on the tufted settee in front of the living room window, nerves doing backflips in her belly. She put her hand over it, remembering there was something in there now. No, not something—*someone.*

She slipped the earbud back in and leaned against the cool glass overlooking the city below. Bexley touched the screen of her phone and scrolled until she found their playlist. There, at the top, was a new song. Her breath caught when she saw the title. *Gypsy Heart.*

She drew in a sharp breath, afraid to play it. Her finger shook as she pressed the Play button. She was shocked when she heard the grainy sound of rain against glass, and then Kai's smooth voice filtered through her earbuds in time with his guitar, sending shivers down her arms.

LAST NIGHT IN LAGUNA

Girl, you have a gypsy heart,
a soul that's all your own.
Been running these dark roads at night,
searching for a home.
Ever since I met you,
I've always been right here,
Waiting for your gypsy heart,
to let go of all its fear.

Cos' we're under the same sky,
nursing the same wounds,
Afraid to love each other,
yet I cannot let you go.
We're under the same sky, darling,
but forever isn't long enough.
I'll never break your gypsy heart,
I'm just longing for your touch.

Tell me when you're tired, girl,
tired of running these roads alone.
My heart is open in your hands,
My heart can be your home.
Wanna feel your light now, darling.

Shine on, let it shine on me.
Need a piece of your heart now, darling.
Shine on, let it shine on me.

We're under the same sky,
Don't slip away again.
Love you, my darling girl.
Please don't let this end.
Wanna feel your light now, darling.
Shine on, let it shine on me.
Need a piece of your heart now, darling.
Shine on, let it shine on me.

Yes, you have a gypsy heart,
But it's beating now for two.
Baby, stop running these dark roads,
When I'm right here waiting for you.

Bexley hadn't realized the tears were falling until she felt a hand on her arm. She jumped and wiped at her face, embarrassed to be caught crying by Mary Jane.

"Go to him," she whispered. "You have to learn to trust, Bexley. Sooner or later, for the sake of that little one, you have to stop running away from your heart."

Bexley nodded, knowing in her heart that MJ was right. She'd never felt this way for a man before; didn't know what to do with the big, old ugly mess of emotions that were swirling around inside of her, as if she drank too much pop at the fair and gotten on the Tilt-a-Whirl. In equal parts she wanted to vomit and get back on to feel the thrill of the ride again.

Hmm. Is this what love feels like?

She had a plan before she saw Kai again. She had a little groveling to do after yesterday's misunderstanding. If she was going to do this, she was going to do it right.

The next morning Bexley knocked hesitantly on Kai's hotel room door. The day was coming up fast, and her heart beat quickly, hope fluttering through like butterflies in chase. She was so afraid to take this leap with Kai, but for the first time, it didn't make her want to run. She was ready to stand with him, face all of these changes together. And there were so many to come.

She wasn't prepared when he opened the door in just a towel, yesterday's five o'clock shadow doubled and his usually vibrant blue eyes flat.

"Hey," Bexley said, suddenly feeling uncertain. "Can I come in?"

"Sure," he said, cracking the door wider to let her step through.

She stopped cold, not all the way in, not completely out. His suitcase was on the bed, mostly packed except for a few toiletries and a pair of jeans and a T-shirt that sat folded on the chair. "You're leaving?"

"Bexley, come in. Let's not stand in the hallway doing this," Kai urged her.

She swallowed. "Doing what? Why are you packing already?"

"I have to get back, Bexley. I dropped everything to get out here to make sure you were okay. But I need to get back and take care of things."

"But, I thought—"

"You thought what, Bex?"

"I thought you wanted to stay? To make this work?" she said, her mouth suddenly dry. She was not going to cry.

"I do, Bexley. But you haven't exactly been the welcoming wagon." He turned away, his back facing her as he sauntered to the chair.

She closed the door behind her just in time. She turned as the towel fell from Kai's waist. Bexley's heart hammered in her chest again, this time from lust, not nerves. He slipped into his jeans, his muscled arms letting the cool black cotton of his T-shirt slide over the hard ridges along his shoulders.

Bexley longed to go over to Kai and reach out to him, let her fingers trace the broad plain of his back. Take him in her arms.

Why was it so hard to be the first one to give? She thought of her mother and father, and all they faced and fought through to be together. No matter how hard things got, they had each other. It didn't matter where they lived or what they had. Family came first. And love was at the heart of it all.

"Kai, I don't want you to go," she whispered.

He turned then, the golden rays of the sunrise coming in through the window and bathing him in light. He didn't run to her as she'd hoped. He stood there—tall, formidable, patient. Waiting, Bexley knew. Waiting on her answer.

She stepped over to the bed and pushed his suitcase aside, sitting down where it had taken up valuable real estate. She folded her legs under her and looked at her hands in her lap before daring to swing her gaze to Kai. His ice blue eyes slammed into her heart when she did, connecting the moment their eyes met. "Kai," she said, her shoulders shaking as the tears were set loose. "There's so much I found out yesterday; so much I need to tell you."

He was next to her side in an instant, the hurt and pride gone from his stance. He sat on the bed and faced her, his hands on either side of her legs. They were so close, but he didn't kiss her. She longed to reach her mouth up to his and find its way home, surrender to the warmth of his lips on hers. Instead, she raised her eyes and met his intense gaze. Home was there too. In the way he looked right into the depths of her.

Her heart felt as if it were breaking right open as she shared every detail that Vaughn had revealed to her the day before. She held nothing back, but recounted the raw, honest truth of it all.

"I'm sorry I didn't come back yesterday. I was in shock—hell, I still am," she admitted, laughing uneasily. "And . . . I needed time to process everything. Everything you offered the day you found out about the baby, and everything I was trying to push away. I needed to figure out *why* I was trying so hard not to let you all the way in."

"Did you figure it out?" Kai asked, brushing his hand through her hair. He sat up straight, looking across the room and out the window at the New York skyline. "Because, you know what, Bexley? I'm not a city guy."

"I know that," she whispered.

"But," he said, and paused, "I would become one for you. With or without the baby, I would become one for you. I'm not gonna lie. The baby makes it easier for me to get my way in this situation, Bex. I've been trying for months to figure out how to get on the same coast as you without freaking you the hell out." He chuckled. "Life has a funny way . . . of helping you out."

Bexley smirked at Kai. "Really? We're having a moment and you pull Alanis Morissette into this?"

"Isn't it ironic?" he asked with a shrug.

She picked up a pillow and playfully whacked him with it. Kai grabbed her wrist and pulled her toward him until their mouths were almost touching. "Bexley, I meant what I said in those song lyrics I sent you yesterday. You have this gypsy soul that I know doesn't need to be tamed. Hell, I love that wild, fiery side to you, and I hope to God you never lose it. I just want to be along for the ride, okay? It does not matter where we go," he said, tucking a stray hair behind her ear and giving her shivers.

"But I'm done just being under the same sky. I want it all, Bex, and I think you do too."

He leaned in and brushed his lips against hers, slowly, softly. "I meant what I said, Bex. I love you," he said, his voice low. "When I went to Laguna that night, I never imagined how my life would change. But you flipped my world upside down. You came in like a wrecking ball—"

Bexley burst out laughing, pushing Kai back onto the bed. "Stop! You are killing me right now." She pinned his arms over his head and kissed him hard, laughter still on her lips. She pulled back slowly, running her hand along the soft cotton that clung to the firm lines of his chest. "I—I've never told anyone I love them before. Outside of my family, I mean. But," she said, patting her stomach, "it looks like we're family now, after all." She smiled shyly down at Kai, and then tugged his arm to get him to sit up.

She looked into those gorgeous blue eyes that she'd lost herself in back in Laguna. And she realized she'd already lost her heart to him, as well. It was time to show him just how much.

She lifted one of his hands and held it against her heart. "Kai, you have been so patient with me. You knocked me off-kilter, too, that night in Laguna. Had me questioning even leaving. If it hadn't been for Vaughn, I might not have. My life has gotten so complicated over the last three months, and it's only going to get harder down the road. But I've come to realize I can't outrun it. I can't run away from everything that scares me. And . . . I deserve my own happiness too," she said quietly.

Bexley smiled, looking down at the firecracker tattoo on his finger. She lifted it to her lips and kissed it. "You had me at this tattoo, Kai. I should've told you sooner. My heart knew then what my mind couldn't quite wrap around. That somehow, in one night, my heart recognized yours. That I was falling in love with you." She lifted her eyes to his again, a shy smile playing on the corner of her lips.

"I love you, Kai. I do."

He arched a brow. "Wow, those words sound so hot coming from your lips, Bexley Rue. I can't wait to hear them for real at the altar."

She placed a hand against his chest. "Slow down now, partner. I've just said I love you for the first time, give me a few more months for the I do's."

His eyebrows shot up in excitement. "But you'll actually

consider them?"

"Yes, I'll actually consider them. I—I already have, actually." She shifted on the bed and reached into her pocket, pulling out her closed hand.

"Kai, with or without this baby, I realized these past few days that I have to have you in my life. All in. On this coast for now, but that doesn't mean that someday we can't head back out west if that's where we belong—together. Because I'm realizing that you're right. I think we're meant to be together."

She shifted on the mattress, her head not quite ready for what she was about to do, but her heart was in a thousand percent. For the first time in her life, her heart was telling her to stay.

chapter Twenty One

There were so many things Kai wanted to say to Bexley. Hell, he was torn between wanting to spill his guts to her and wanting to kiss that gorgeous mouth of hers and silencing them both for the next hour.

Well—not completely silencing them.

But he could tell how hard this was for Bexley. He saw the pain written across her face when she'd told him about her parents and Vaughn. There was nothing he could do to change her family's past, but he could do everything to give her—and their baby—the future they deserved. She was right about one thing. The key word was *together*.

Yes, he'd been packing up to head back to California, but it was simply so he could tidy up the loose ends of his life there before moving to the East Coast for good. He loved Sonoma and being near his family, but Bexley was his family now, too, and she and the baby would always come first now.

A baby. *Holy crap! I'm gonna be a father.*

"Kai, everyone thinks that having a gypsy heart means I was running away from something. And, yeah, there's some truth to that. But you're the first person who really understands me, who seems to get that maybe all this time I wasn't running *from* something, but running toward the possibility of something better that was meant to be. Maybe all this time I was running to get to you."

Bexley blushed a little when she said that, but her jade green eyes stayed focused on him, never wavering. "I'm ready, Kai. I want us to figure out how to make this work—if you'll be patient with me. My sister is dying, and she's slipping away faster than we ever could have imagined," Bexley said, wiping her eyes. "I know there will be times when I'll want to tuck tail and run again, or hide under the weight of it all."

She took a deep breath and opened her palm. There, nestled in the center of her hand, were two rings, not traditional in any sense of the word—just like Bexley. The rings matched and had three smooth layers fused together, one on top of the other: wood, turquoise, and titanium. They were stunning works of art and Kai's heart hitched at what Bexley was doing holding onto them.

"Bex—" Kai started.

"Kai . . . just hear me out. I'm not asking you to marry me—yet. I'm just asking for you to come back to New York with that intention. Consider these promise rings. When I say I'm all in, I mean I'm all in. And I need to know that we're on the same page. Because I can't have my heart broken again. I lost my parents, and I'm about to lose my sister. I can't lose you too," she said, small tears sliding silently down her cheek.

"I love you, Kai. I don't ever want to think about walking away from you again. So, will you wear this ring and help me stop running these dark roads alone? My heart is in your hands, and my heart can be your home. I want to let my light shine down on you—whatever the heck that actually means," Bexley said, smiling.

Kai scoffed. "Did you just quote one of my songs, and then make fun of it, all in one breath?"

"Of course not," Bexley teased before getting serious again. "Read the inscriptions."

Kai picked up the two rings. He flipped over the smaller one and read: *Take on me*. Then he flipped over the larger ring and read: *Take me on*. A smile spread across his face as he remembered the moment in the tree house when he picked this song for her to listen to. It was about leaving, but asking the other to take a risk on love—a gentle hint that he didn't want their time together to end after their one night in Laguna.

"I was shying away, but you came for me anyway," Bexley said, grinning.

"It's no better to be safe than sorry," Kai deadpanned.

Bexley's dimples flashed, rewarding Kai with their sexiness. She leaned in and took the larger of the two rings from his hand. She slid it onto his long, thick ring finger, pleased that the ring fit perfectly—thanks to his cousin Josh's help. She placed both hands on the sides of Kai's face and kissed him slowly, with heat and promise.

Kai pulled back, holding up the dainty matching ring. She wiggled her hand out and let him slide the small ring onto her finger, before he laced his hand with her own. "Bexley, I swear you have made me the happiest man alive in New York just now. I was so scared I was going to lose you when you didn't call or come by yesterday."

"I'm sorry, Kai. I just needed to get my head on straight—take it all in. Needed to find my true north. I've been moving around for so long I forgot which way was home. Now that I found you, now that we'll always be under the same sky together, I'll never lose sight again. I promise."

Kai wrapped his hands around the back of Bexley's head and pulled her in for a kiss that he knew would leave her toes curled and have them celebrating in bed all day long. He had every intention of making good on these promise rings, and replacing them with diamonds for her someday. Someday really soon.

extra special recognition

Elements of Kaira Rouda's Laguna Beach have been included in this story (*Last Night in Laguna*) with the express permission of Kaira Rouda.

Laguna Beach by Kaira Rouda

Laguna Beach is a sexy modern romance series by author Kaira Rouda, set in beautiful Laguna Beach, California. The stories feature the cast of a high school-based reality TV show, ten years after the show wrapped. Inspired by the original reality show, Laguna Beach: The Real Orange County, the *Laguna Beach* series is beach reading at its best.

Laguna Nights
Laguna Heights
Laguna Lights
Laguna Sights
Laguna Dreams

more books by
C.M. ALBERT

FAITH IN LOVE *(Arden's Glen Romance series – book one)*
Full of grief and jaded by love, corporate philanthropist Egan MacGuire is given two options by his boss: take a leave of absence or kiss his job goodbye. A road trip with a friend is just the distraction Egan needs to figure out how to get his life back on track. Celeste St. Angelo left the bright lights and big city for the mountains of North Carolina to open the next phase of her flourishing Angel Therapy business, a healing and wellness center. With the grand opening looming she has no time for distractions, especially love. When divine timing sparks an unexpected romance, will Egan and Celeste be able to leave their troubled pasts behind and find the courage to have a little faith in love?

PROOF OF LOVE *(Arden's Glen Romance series – book two)*
Dez Wright bed hops because it's easier to let a man between her legs than into her heart. After the death of her high school sweetheart in a motorcycle accident that leaves Dez with a bum knee and a shattered heart, she throws all of her passion and energy into something that can't hurt her: her flourishing photography career. Mitch Michaelson thought he was dead the

day he wrestled a pissed-off shark snorkeling off the Hawaiian coast with a model whose name he can hardly remember. But the tryst in paradise cost him more than his arm; it destroyed his career as a famous iron sculptor. After years of intense therapy, Mitch is finally rebuilding a new life working with kids at the community center in his sleepy North Carolina town. When Dez blows into Arden's Glen looking to take his picture for some do-gooder coffee table book, Mitch wants no part of it. He's put his glamorous past where it belongs and wants nothing more than to lay low, help the kids in his community, and be left alone. When fate steps in and brings the two together to help their friends and a troubled kid in need, will a couple of photographs and a magical one-night stand be all the proof of love they need? Or will their two stubborn hearts stay hell-bent on keeping their walls in place and playing it safe forever?

THE WHITE ROOM *(Genre: Steamy contemporary romance)*
The rules are simple: No Names. No Commitments. Two hours. They're put into place to protect us—exclusive clients lucky enough to afford the cost of playing. But everyone knows some rules are made to be broken. When hearts and bodies collide, even the best intentions slip away . . . exposing the real reasons why we seek the White Room in the first place. Will the White Room set you free? Step inside and find yourself.

about the author

USA Today Bestselling Author C.M. Albert writes heartwarming romances that are both "sexy and flirty, sweet and dirty"! Her writing infuses a healthy blend of humor, inspiration, and romance. She's a sucker for a good villain, and a die-hard believer in everlasting love. In her spare time, she and her husband wrangle their two kids and enjoy spending time outdoors. When not writing or kid wrangling, C.M. Albert is also a Certified Medical Reiki Master, chocolate chip cookie aficionado, kindness ambassador, and seeker of naps. You can stay in touch with C.M. Albert or join her online at:

Website: www.colleenalbert.com
Amazon: www.amazon.com/C.M.-Albert
Facebook: www.facebook.com/cmalbertwrites
Colleen's Angels Street Team & Beta Reader Group:
www.facebook.com/groups/1015040795184238
The Official C.M. Albert Fan Club:
www.facebook.com/groups/602979050062067
Instagram: www.instagram.com/cmalbertwrites
Twitter: www.twitter.com/colleenmalbert
Newsletter: http://eepurl.com/b6jIsz
Email: colleenalbert@icloud.com

Made in the USA
Monee, IL
17 March 2021